SEDUCTION, DECEIT & A SLICE OF APPLE PIE

Cover design by Andrea Walters

Published in the United States.

Join Allison on Facebook.com/AllisonJJanda
Follow her on Twitter @AllisonJanda
And visit AllisonJanda.com for excerpts, updates and more!

Don't miss the first novel in the
Marian Moyer mystery series:

Sex, Murder & Killer Cupcakes

This book is dedicated, with utmost love and appreciation, to Lindsey Rai and Kali. Thank you for always being by my side, no matter the situation.

Things had started out innocently enough. The promise of dinner and a movie that night. Around high noon, Addison called me in a panic. Addison in a panic is nothing unusual but, as it turns out, it was warranted this time around. Our main model for the January issue of *Food Porn* had come down with Salmonella poisoning. We'd already pushed the shoot back by a week and couldn't afford to lose more time. Deadline was looming. Rory, our resident layout guru, needed photos yesterday. After a few seconds of freaking out myself, I decided to make a call to my date that night. Devilishly handsome James Holden was a hot commodity in Milwaukee these days. He'd be good for business. Assuming, of course, he'd agree to strip down nearly naked to pose with a slice of apple pie from the new bakery around the corner. It's amazing what a man will do for a woman when he's head over heels for her. I'd barely gotten halfway through my speech before he'd agreed to be in my studio by 6pm.

His hair and makeup took less than ten minutes. I'm telling you, the man is a looker. Barely there James, who I was pretty sure had never modeled before this moment, blew me away. He was born to be behind a camera. It's too bad his face is lost in the world of private investigation.

Not so much lost, I suppose, as under appreciated. His body rippled with muscles, a slight tan and gorgeous gatherings of freckles across his shoulders and chest. I was so smitten, I'm surprised I remembered how to work the camera.

Somehow, I made it through the shoot without throwing myself at him. Amazing, considering the numerous fantasies that spun through my head with every flash of the camera. After depositing the flash drive into Rory's eager hands, and allowing James a chance to put some clothes back on, we raced through an obligatory dinner, squirmed our way through the latest flick at the local cinema, and sped back to my apartment. Well, I definitely sped, but he made it first, so I'm assuming he'd been in a hurry, too.

We'd both acted nonchalant in my quaint apartment. Kept up some casual conversation that had nothing to do with what we were each really thinking. As I was opening a bottle of wine, I turned to ask him another lame question. He took the bottle from my hands and pressed up against me. I felt the hard, cold granite press into my lower back as I was trapped between my kitchen counter and James's rock-solid body. His green eyes gazed directly into mine as I gently caressed my hand against his soft, reddish-brown hair. My hand came to a rest behind his neck, but I stopped myself from going a step further and pulling him in for a kiss. I'd let him do the honors if he was so inclined.

A shiver coursed through my body as he continued to study me. His eyes floated from my face, to my neck, to my blouse, which may have been slightly more unbuttoned than could be considered appropriate. We'd been dating for just over a month and while we'd had some wildly amazing make-out sessions, we hadn't yet done the deed. I felt his pelvis grind hard against my own. He planted a hand on the counter on either side of me, then leaned in and began to kiss my neck, trailing his lips slowly down to my collarbone, which he licked softly. A small sigh escaped my lips as my hand curled up into his hair and grabbed hold tightly. I felt my knees shaking as my legs threatened to give out. Good thing the counter was behind me, or I'd have been a puddle on the floor, for sure. Nothing else could have kept me from falling.

As his lips slowly made their way up my neck and towards my ear, I took a sharp breath. My whole body felt tingly as he sighed softly against the lobe and then slowly, gently, took it into his mouth. Like a scene from "Gone with the Wind," I threw my free arm around his shoulder for support and allowed myself to moan in ecstasy. I had become the women I'd read about in Harlequin romance novels and James was straight off of one of their covers. You really haven't lived until someone has sucked your earlobe. You just — "Oh. My. God." I whispered, as his hands began to wander lazily, but skillfully, to the button of my jeans.

I felt his index finger tuck into the waistband followed by the warmth of his touch. His free hand tugged softly at my shirt before slowly, sneakily, making its way underneath of it. His left hand continued to gently play with my waistband while his right had moved from the counter and was now stalled on my hip, gently caressing it. Slowly, his grip tightened and he pulled my pelvis towards him, at the same time popping open the top button of my jeans. I gasped. "Um-" Looking up into his eyes, which had become liquid pools of desire, I swallowed impossibly hard. His hand was now toying with the band of my panties, which were boring blue and white striped high cotton briefs from the department store. I'd worn them in an effort to keep myself from doing anything stupid. I had also failed to shave my legs, hoping that, that would deter things as well. "I don't think that we should-." The hand that had been gripping my waist moved higher and began to trace the outline of my bra through my thin cotton shirt. Thankfully, that at least, was slightly classier, with shimmery blue lace. I felt my breath quicken. Things were going downhill fast. While a normal woman would have been thanking her lucky stars, I could only panic.

James's hand moved deftly to the clasp of my bra, which unsnapped itself quickly. I'd bought it for that purpose and found myself regretting the decision. Suddenly, both of his hands were unbuttoning what was left of the buttons on my blouse. In one swift tug, it was off my arms, hanging limply from my wrists. Another tug and the blouse was on the floor. "Wait, wait wait-" I said, just as he began to ease off my bra. With a wicked smile, he held his hands up in defeat, but began to slowly nip and kiss the peaks of my breasts. Without warning, he had picked me up and was carrying me towards the living room couch. I clutched at my bra, desperate to keep it from falling down any further.

"I have seen those," he said, playfully referring to the time I'd gotten naked in the back of his car outside a coffee shop. James Holden may have taken my virginity, but he wouldn't take away my dignity. Again.

Gently, he placed me on my overstuffed two-seater and tugged his own shirt off over his head. Dropping it to the ground, he moved in closer. Kissing me, he slowly pushed me down into a horizontal position on the couch. I found my hands running slowly over his broad, freckled shoulders. His hands stroked my hair and face softly, but he didn't make a move to do away with my bra, which just barely covered my breasts. "James?" I asked softly.

"Hmmm?"

"Do you- is this- I mean-"

He gently placed a finger over my lips. "We're not doing anything you don't want to do," he promised.

Damn it. Just like a man. Getting me all hot and bothered before doing the gentlemanly thing in letting me decide our course of action — or lack thereof. I wriggled beneath him and found myself grinding against his body. He clutched my hair and sucked in a breath. "Careful, Moyer."

I sighed. "It's not that I don't want to."

He face grew dark. "I know," he assured me. Pushing himself into a sitting position, he reached for his shirt, which lay sadly on the wooden floor next to the couch. Pulling it over his head, he leaned down to give me another quick kiss. "I guess I should go then."

Alarms began to go off in my brain. As well as other areas. I was surprised that my body wasn't smoking. "You can stay-" I offered weakly, clutching my bra tightly against my chest. I felt like an idiot. A hot and bothered idiot, but an idiot nonetheless. Why had I said anything about the elephant in the room that neither of us was able to ignore?

James dropped his gaze from my face, to my neck, to my chest, to my stomach, to the open fly on my jeans. I tried hard not to fidget under his penetrating stare. His hands gently caressed my exposed hip bone before he growled and pulled himself away. "Can't," he muttered. Standing, he shifted his pants and walked quickly for the front door of my apartment. "I'll call you tomorrow," he promised. The door shut quietly behind him.

"Bye," I whispered to no one. After a moment, I rose from the couch, still clutching my bra, and shuffled towards the front door. Before locking the deadbolt, I peered through the peephole. James was still standing in the hallway, gently banging his head against the cream-colored wall opposite my door. With a huge sigh, he again adjusted his nether regions and began walking slowly towards the elevators, hands shoved deep in his pockets, head down like a kid who'd just lost his puppy.

Feeling defeated myself, I clicked the lock into place and

made my way back to my bedroom. Peeling off the rest of my date night clothes and jewelry, I went to my dark wooden dresser and pulled out a long-sleeved thigh-length flannel shirt and a pair of long, fuzzy socks. Not the fuzzy pink pair that held my incredibly large gun. Another pair. I own a lot of fuzzy socks. Fluffing my curls tiredly, I made my way into the bathroom to wash my face.

About a month ago, I'd made the decision to date two very different, yet equally gorgeous, intriguing men. They had both done their part in saving my life, despite the fact that at one (or several) times throughout the course of a murder investigation, I thought they were both trying to kill me themselves.

James Holden had been my college crush, my first love. My first — well, a lot of things. As it turned out, he was a self-made millionaire, having started his own private investigation company with his (silent) partner in crime, Mika Andrushkiv. The two had been friends for many years, but when Mika decided to take his investments and split for warmer weather than Wisconsin offered, they had lost touch. A while back, Mika was pulled from retirement to help James pin down a slippery son of a gun by the name of Barry. Barry had been out to kill me.

I run a highly successful magazine, from which I make very paltry money. It's a long story, but suffice to say, I'm incredibly happy and wouldn't change a thing. As it turns out, Barry had longed for me to launch his modeling career. When a year, three years, five years, and then nearly ten years passed without me inviting him to model for my magazine, *Food Porn,* he went off the deep end. I guess for those of us who are fairly well mentally balanced, we'd just get a new dream. Barry, on the other hand, hatched an elaborate plot to kill me, that had involved buying a bakery as a cover. Luckily, he'd used James as an investor. James the private investigator. Stupid on Barry's part, but I guess everyone makes mistakes. Once Barry's plan started to near its finale, James drug Mika back to Wisconsin to act as an undercover agent. Unbeknownst to myself, my partner and best friend Addison, and our good friend and *Food Porn* Marketing Director, Rory, we hired Mika as our newest "model" at just the right time.

Mika and I fell for one another about the same time James realized he had feelings for me beyond a quickie in the back of his first car out of college. The two had decided that, because they were no longer close enough to be considered good friends, they'd both work towards winning my affection. Mika officially moved back to Wisconsin about two weeks ago. No longer James's secret partner, he'd started his own PI firm. Needless to say, the two were in very high demand, especially amongst the ladies. Still, I wasn't the least bit concerned that either would stray before I made up my mind. Frankly, I find the whole thing rather unbelievable myself. It has been just over a month and I'm still trying to make up my mind. I know I need to decide soon and put one man out of his misery. It's only fair.

My face dripping with cool water, I reached for a towel and patted my skin dry before opening my eyes to look in the mirror. I was above average looking. My skin a pale peach, my dark gray eyes slightly smaller than I would have liked. My lips were the perfect plumpness, my nose not the slightest bit upturned. While I wasn't overweight, I certainly wasn't model skinny and preferred peanut butter cups to Wheat Thins. Perhaps my most distinguished feature, however, was my thick, curly, auburn hair that fell to just below my shoulders. Blowing a strand of it off of my face, I squared my shoulders and made my way back out into the living room, alone.

Before heading to the kitchen to snatch a Reese's out of my freezer, I strode over to Fred's tank. Fred is my red betta fish. He's not the most protective of pets, but his silent stare speaks volumes when I'm trying to make a decision. Pinching a bit of food between my fingers, I dropped it into his tank and watched as he quickly zipped to the surface and started eating. I watched him for a few moments. "Wish I had your problems," I muttered finally. I found myself wondering if Fred would be considered a stud by betta standards.

I was so lost in thought that I almost didn't hear the familiar ring of my cell phone. I made my way to the kitchen, where it was miraculously being charged. Checking the caller ID, I answered quickly. "Hey," I said, walking towards the fridge and pulling out a gallon of milk.

"Hey," Addison answered. I could hear her hand muffle

the receiver as she loudly called, "you owe me dinner!" More scratching as she removed her hand. "Sorry," she continued apologetically.

As I poured a thick stream of milk into a glass, I frowned. "Why does Rory owe you dinner?"

Rory and Addison had started dating back when things had just gotten weird around the office. Their togetherness had made everything that much weirder. Addison resembled a bustier, curvier Cameron Diaz. She was smart as a whip, in-your-face sexual and she always spoke her mind. I guess she had to, considering that she worked full time for the local paper and was constantly being nominated for prestigious journalistic awards. Rory, meanwhile, was well over six feet tall, lanky, pale and wore thick-rimmed glasses straight out of a sitcom. He was adorably awkward, nerdy and everything that Addison was not. He was also partial to clothes that were slightly too long or just a hair too short. Still, you'd never meet a more loyal man, nor one better at designing magazine layouts. Surprisingly, his apartment was lavishly decorated and Rory himself was fabulously wealthy. He just chose comfort over Calvin Klein. Rory had also been in love with Addie since day one. She'd taken a little longer to warm up to him, having dated a steady stream of losers since college. Odd together though they were, they were still somehow just right.

"Well, Rory said that you were going to get laid tonight. I have my money on you doing the oompa loompa with

Mika first."

I wrinkled my nose and put the milk jug back into the fridge before opening the freezer and pulling from my stash of Reese's Peanut Butter Cups. "First of all, never call it that again," I chided her. "Second of all, what makes you think I won't get laid tonight?"

Despite the fact that she lived on the opposite side of town, I just knew she was rolling her eyes. "Please," she answered. "You wouldn't be answering the phone if you were in the middle of something."

"Maybe we're finished."

"In which case you definitely should have gone with Mika," she teased.

We laughed and chatted for a few minutes about the date that never really was. Addison was fascinated by the idea of James posing with nothing much more than apple pie and demanded to see photographic evidence immediately. After we'd discussed what had transpired after the shoot, I growled in frustration. "Why can't I just- just- go for it?" I asked her. "We have been together before. In that way."

"True," she responded. "But this time it is going to mean something. Especially considering that whether it is with James or Mika, sex with one probably means lights out for the other relationship. In your case anyway."

I nodded. She was correct on that one. I was a one-man Sally. "I just don't know which one I like more."

"Pros and cons. James. Go!"

"Well-" I hesitated. "James is- masculine," I told her.

"And his biceps are huge. Like almost the size of my head."

"You do like arms."

"Mmm. And his eyes- I just get lost in them." I thought hard for a moment. "He's such a decision maker. He acts quickly. I believe every single word that he says."

"But?"

"I never know what he's thinking. He doesn't talk very much, I feel like I'm prying conversations from him sometimes." I paused. "He also feels dangerous. Not like he is dangerous, but more like he draws in the danger. Does that even make sense?"

"He's in a rough line of business," Addison agreed. "What about Mika?"

I closed my eyes and summoned the gorgeous Ukrainian to my mind. Imagining his dark curls and blue eyes made me shiver involuntarily. He and I had done a photo shoot as well, several weeks ago. He'd had just as much pull over me as James had. Possibly even more. "He just...is," I shrugged. "I can't explain it. It just works. Not because there's a good reason, but just because it does."

Addison giggled. "What about cons?"

I thought hard. "Mika would want to leave Wisconsin eventually," I admitted.

"You're positive?"

"Well, no. But it makes sense, considering the only reason he moved up here from the Bahamas or wherever was to date me." Sighing, I admitted, "I really don't know that he has that many flaws. Our conversations are perfect, other than the fact that half the time I'm totally tongue-tied. He pulls out my chair. He helps me into my coat. He cooks me dinner. He calls just to say 'hi.' He hung the new curtains I bought last week."

"How do they look?"

I studied the brown, velvety curtains that just barely skimmed my light wooden floors. A large blue and gray area rug, also new, was pushed right up against the floor length windows. I'd changed apartments annually ever since I graduated college. This was the first place I'd lived that felt like home. I wanted to make it look like one, too. I'd finally purchased my first set of curtains and my first area rug just last week. Baby steps. "They're alright," I told her. "I need to leave them up a bit longer to decide how I really feel about them."

"When do you see Mika again?" she asked.

"Not until next week," I groaned, cradling the phone between my shoulder and my ear as I carried my glass of milk and an orange Reese's packet into the living room. "He's out of town doing some casework."

"Did he tell you what it was?" she asked hopefully. Always the reporter. She'd had a sensational hit when the story of Barry broke, but the last few weeks had been quiet and she was itching for another success before award nominations were due for winter quarter.

"Of course not," I scoffed.

"Nothing wrong with asking," she muttered. "So since you're not getting laid tonight, what are you up to?"

I eyed the television control and as quietly as possible, opened my candy. "Plenty," I answered sarcastically between chews. "Just rolling in offers and activity over here."

"Did you want to go out?"

I looked dejectedly at my pajamas. "I just changed."

"Want company? We can watch a movie."

"You're with Rory!"

"He understands," she responded. "Right?" she called out to him.

"Of course, dear," he answered.

"See you in 20?" she asked.

"I'll leave the front door unlocked."

"Pick a good flick. The last one you chose- what was it?"

"The Rogue Hunter?"

"That's it. It was awful."

I giggled and promised to be more careful this time around. Hanging up the phone and tossing it onto the ottoman, I reached for the television control, clicked "main menu" and flipped over to the newly-released movies screen. Scrolling through, I settled on the latest film featuring a blond-haired, blue-eyed actress who had modeled for *Food Porn* in January's feature review. She'd been posing with Sweeties, a new fruit that was a cross between an apple and a pear. The woman had needed more than a few fruits to hide her ample bosom as she posed in her leafy Eve-inspired panties, but the final results had shot our circulation sky-high. And anyway, I wasn't much in the mood for having to figure out a plot line. I wanted to understand how it ended without having to use much of my brain.

Pushing myself off the couch, I went to unlock the front door before going over to the closet and pulling out some extra pillows and blankets. Setting them on the couch, I trailed into the kitchen and uncorked a bottle of wine before scrounging through the cabinets for a box of microwave popcorn, which I just knew had to be in there someplace.

I had just popped the bag into the microwave when I heard the front door squeak open. "I'm in the kitchen," I hollered. I heard the door close and footsteps echo in the entry hall. "That was fast, Addison," I added. "I thought I had at least another ten minutes to prep."

"It's not Addison," came the response.

I froze. My thoughts immediately turned to my gun, tucked deep in the trenches of my sock drawer. There was no way I'd be able to get there before this loon attacked me. Besides, I'd pulled all of the bullets out of it. I wasn't very into the idea of shooting people, even if they did want me dead. I'd long hoped that the time would never again come when I'd need the gun. Additionally I'd wished that if and when that day did arrive, the gun itself would be terrifying enough to scare off an attacker. It was a pretty serious looking weapon. Besides, stranger things had happened, right?

"Sugar?"

I felt the tension instantly leave my body. Turning quickly, I smiled. "You're back early." Mika grinned and held out his arms to me. I practically ran to him. "You scared me."

"What are you doing leaving your door unlocked?" he asked, teasingly. "Haven't you had enough close calls?"

"Addison is going to be here any minute," I said into his soft, red flannel button down. He smelled like soap and spicy aftershave. I could have breathed him in all night. I'd never found flannel, especially red flannel, to be very sexy before Mika and I had started dating. I chalked it up to something a logger would wear. How very wrong I was. I now even owned a few flannels myself — exhibit one, my pajamas. "We're having a girls' night."

"A girls' night," he whispered in his gentle, lilting accent, pulling me close and resting his chin atop my head. "I was hoping to get you all to myself tonight."

Then it's a good thing you didn't get here about 20 minutes ago, I thought. A shiver went through me as I remembered where my night with James had led. I wondered if either of them had spotted each other.

"Cold?" Mika asked, hugging me slightly tighter. I let my hands wander aimlessly up and down his lanky, muscular back. He was much thinner and taller in frame than James, but no less attractive. Mika growled quietly in my ear. "How long until Addison gets here?"

I giggled and gently pulled away. "Soon."

"How soon?"

"Too soon."

Jokingly, he harrumphed and wandered into the kitchen. I watched him, biting my lower lip as I imagined what was under his outfit, as he rounded the counter and looked at the bottle of wine that I'd uncorked. I'd seen it all once before, his incredibly sexy body, during the photo shoot we'd done together last month, but there was nothing wrong with hoping to see it again. And again and again and again. With an approving nod, he turned to me after reading the wine label. "I've been teaching you well."

I laughed. "I did drink wine before you came around."

"Nothing that was very good," he teased.

"You didn't either. It's been a learning process."

He smiled a little and I felt faint. When he smiled full-wattage, I pretty much fell to my knees and cried. He seemed aware of his allure among women and always kept his grins fairly minimal. My knees buckled just then in an attempt to remain upright, but all I wanted to do was swoon. His dimples were out of this world. "Touché," he whispered. There was a brief moment when I thought he might sweep towards me, take me in his arms and kiss me, dipping me low towards the ground, but it passed when we heard the front door click open.

"Hello!" Addison called out in her singsong voice. I heard her boots thump as she pulled them off and dropped them onto the hard entryway floor. They were probably something high fashion with heels. If anyone could find high-heeled boots and walk in them properly in snow, it was Addison. Cold was not an excuse for her to look dowdy like the rest of the Midwestern population in the middle of winter. "I hope you've already used your bathroom, because I still hate the idea of using Rory's when I need to p- hello, Mika!" Her cheeks had begun to pink in embarrassment, but her smile remained tight. She shifted her gaze from him to me and then back to Mika. "I thought you were out of town on business."

"I was," he answered, the upper corner of his lip tugging slightly. "I got back early and thought I'd surprise Em, but it sounds like the two of you already have plans tonight."

I saw Addison's eyes grow worried, though she didn't drop the tight, pinched smile from her face. "How long have you been here?" she asked, practically through gritted teeth

Mika's head tilted sideways in confusion, so I stepped in to answer. "Not long," I assured her. She was clearly concerned he'd run into James. While both men knew that I was dating the other, it wasn't something we opted to bring up in everyday conversation. I told you — the elephant in the room. "After you called."

She nodded. "Well. Good to see you, Mika."

He was still staring at her confused but became aware that she wouldn't be sharing any additional information. "Good to see you, too. I was just saying to Marian that I had to get going. A few things I need to go over yet tonight at the office." He strode over to my side and gently pulled me to him by my hip. Kissing me softly on the head, he whispered, "call me tomorrow when you're free?"

I nodded and walked him to the door. "We'll catch up soon, too," he called over his shoulder to Addie. The two had been to lunch once or twice. Anyone who wanted to get to me had to go through Addison. She had yet to ask James out for coffee and I suspected it was because she'd already been swayed to Team Ukraine.

"Sure thing!" she called back weakly, adding a pitiful wave which he couldn't see.

Once the door had closed and I was walking back into the living room, she rushed over and clutched my arm.

"Oh. My. GOD." she hissed, walking with me towards the kitchen. "You could have warned me he was going to be here. I'm mortified!"

"Sorry, girl," I responded, reaching for the wine bottle. "He just showed up. The door was unlocked. He walked right in. Scared the crap out of me."

"You really should be more careful," she admonished. "Who knows what could just walk in off of the street." She paused. "You need to move to a building with a doorman. Or at least, someplace that has a security camera."

I shrugged and handed her a glass of wine, which she gulped at gratefully. "But I'm really happy here. And anyway, Barry's in prison for a long time," I responded.

"Yes, but with your line of work..."

"Which?" I asked. In addition to taking photographs for *Food Porn,* I also moonlit as a crime scene photographer for the police department. Granted, those subjects were usually already dead and didn't give me much to worry about, other than what their blood spatter patterns meant in regard to their death. I wasn't a blood spatter analyst by any means, but I'd photographed various deaths and blood patterns over the years enough to have an idea of what most of them suggested crime-wise. But don't go getting me to nerd out on that.

"Either," she chided, setting her wine glass on the table. "I love having security cameras in my building."

"Yes, but you're a reporter. A really good one that exposes a lot of underground crime among the city elite.

Half of the city hates you."

"The other half doesn't care, they just want into my pants."

"Even the ones that hate you want into your pants," I teased.

She gave me a withering glare. Addison had never slept with the higher ups for a chance at success. It just wasn't her. Still, that didn't stop Addie from using her body to get her way. The girl gave killer neck massages. I'm not sure I want to know how many of those she has passed out for free. "I'm just saying that having a security camera is beneficial to those of us working in the industries that we do. And now I'm going to use your bathroom before I completely ruin your brand new rug."

A few minutes later, the two of us were sitting on my couch holding our wine glasses, sharing a large bowl of freshly-popped buttered popcorn. Addison was dressed in one of my oversized t-shirts and my longest pair of sweatpants, which were still slightly too short for her, ending just above the ankle. I reached for the control to start the movie, but she stopped me. "Oh, now," she teased. "We have a lot to talk about before we go watching our featured star save New York City."

I gulped. "Like what?" I asked, taking a long, lingering sip of sweet white wine. I was hoping to avoid additional conversations about my personal life until I managed to get it sorted out.

"Like what would have happened with Mika had I not

shown up tonight?"

"Nothing!" I cried. Addison eyed me suspiciously as she sipped from her glass, arching an eyebrow as she did so. "Well," I said after a moment. "Maybe something."

"When were the two of you together last?"

"A few days ago. The night before he left town."

"Oh, that's right. I haven't heard about any of this," she said, clutching her blankets tightly and leaning in closer. Her eyes were sparkling with excitement.

"It's your own fault for working so much."

She flipped her hair. "Someone needs to tell the citizens what a money-grubbing peacock their potential mayoral candidate is. I've had to keep tabs on the guy all week. I'm also positive he's knee-deep in an affair; he just hasn't tripped up yet. He will, though. They always do." We sat in silence for a moment, both likely pondering how corrupt figures ever made it into office, before Addison shook out of her reverie. "So?" she asked, interrupting my line of thought.

"Well, hold on," I responded. "I haven't gotten any updates on you and Rory in weeks."

"We've already taken full advantage of each other," she answered. "You know all about that. Besides, what do you want me to tell you? That when Rory gets really turned on, he kind of moans a little bit? That he has a huge, throbbing-"

"Okay!" I cried, nearly dropping my wine glass in an attempt to cover my ears. "I don't want to hear about

Rory's huge, throbbing anything." I'd known Rory for years, on a purely brotherly/sisterly love basis. He was a brilliant marketing man. A real sweetheart. A total geek. I wasn't the least bit sexually attracted to him.

Addison grinned wickedly. "Back to you, I suppose," she prompted. "What happened the night before Mika left town?"

I sunk back into the couch cushions, which enveloped me lovingly as I sipped my wine. My stomach fluttered and I drew upon my memories of that day just before Mika had skipped town for a new case he'd taken on in Minneapolis. He'd actually taken me on a date to see The Domes. I'd lived in Milwaukee for years but had never visited the historical landmark. They were a warm welcome against winter's bitter cold temperatures. After that, we'd had a long dinner, where we lingered over dessert and wine for hours afterwards. However, it was when he dropped me off at my apartment that things really heated up.

He'd parked out front, per usual, and moved in slowly for our end-of-night kiss. The kiss eventually led to necking, which eventually led to him hauling me across the armrest and into his lap, where I continued to get lost in both his eyes and his lips for the next several minutes. Once the car windows were sufficiently steamed, I let myself out of the driver's side door, stumbling into the slick street. I'd intended to say goodnight there, but he followed me into the inky black night and kissed me again, forcing me up against his Jeep. This time, it was so deep, so passionate, that I completely forgot I was standing outside in sub-zero temperatures. When he pulled away, my eyes were still closed, my lips still poised for one last smooch. My legs had turned to jelly and the only thing keeping me upright was the cool exterior of Mika's Jeep. He'd chuckled and whispered, "I think that's sufficient for tonight," before walking me to the front door of the lobby.

"You can come up," I'd offered, the words flying out of my mouth with little care to consequence.

He'd hesitated. "It's not that I don't want to."

I'd been taken aback by his answer. Hadn't he just been all over me? Suddenly, I'd remembered just how much rejection could sting and exactly why I'd all but stopped dating in the months and years leading up to the past month. Men were cruel. I'd never had a decent experience. No wonder I'd become a workaholic. I didn't have time for this kind of crap. "Well," I had said, lowering my head so that I was staring at my shoes while blinking rapidly to ward of tears. "Goodnight, then."

He'd grabbed for my arm as I'd begun to walk away. "Marian," he said sternly. I'd clenched my jaw but had refused to make eye contact. "Marian, don't do that. I do like you."

"So it's because you like me that you don't want to come upstairs. Why, I've never heard that one before," I snarled sarcastically. Raising my chin, all traces of tears gone, I had stared deeply into his seductive baby blues, swallowing hard and willing myself not to give in and start kissing him all over again. I wouldn't be the one to make the move. Not after I'd just laid all of my cards on the table and he'd shot me down with a full house.

"I really like this side of you," he whispered, cupping my chin in his hand and pulling me in for another kiss. Lord help me, I kissed him back. "Willful. Stubborn. It's pretty sexy," he continued, pulling away.

I'd stood helpless, arms limp at my sides, wishing he'd just shut up and leave or shut up and kiss me until the sun rose, which, from the looks of it, would be happening fairly soon. "So what's the problem?" I asked.

"I can't sleep with you when you're seeing somebody else," he shrugged assured. "Even though James and I aren't great friends any more, we were partners once. He's a good man. I respect him. I also respect you and your decision, whatever it is going to be. I'm not dating you to earn a quick trip down your pants." He kissed my forehead. "Don't you think for a second that I don't want you," he added. "Don't feel like you're the only one in this situation experiencing rejection."

He had me there. With that, he'd given me one last long, lingering kiss and then turned, striding quickly back to his car. "Wait," I'd called. He stopped and turned, staring at me curiously. I jogged over and threw myself into his arms. He hugged me tightly and when we parted, I kissed him one last time before running inside. I watched from the lobby as he crawled back into his car and saw the steam rise from the tailpipe in the cold, blustery pre-dawn, pressed my forehead to the glass front door and waved as he'd driven away. Sighing, I turned and drug myself slowly towards the elevator. They just didn't make men here like they made them in the Ukraine, it would seem.

I recounted every single detail of the evening for Addison. When I finished, she sighed deeply and almost melted into the couch. "Is that man for real?" she asked. "I mean for real, for real?"

"Sure seems like it," I replied, rolling to my side to face her. "But do you think he's serious? Or was he just saying that so that he doesn't have to see me naked?" I patted my small, but definitely not firm, belly and took another sip of empty calories from my wine glass. I may have over poured us by a good three ounces each.

"Oh, stop," she scolded. "You're going on as if you're Monstro The Whale."

"Well, anyway," I continued on, ignoring her. "I haven't slept with either one of them. Yet."

"Then," she said, tucking a foot under her thigh, "take it all for what it's worth. You're an independent woman. You've called your own shots for a long time. From what you've told me, they both sound like the types to fall at your feet with whatever you request. Just depends on whose approach you like more." She paused. "You're always taking care of everyone, Marian. You always have. While I can't say I haven't liked some of your past beaus, I can't say I felt they deserved you." I laughed, but Addison remained serious. "I've always seen you being with someone who could take care of you. Not take away your autonomy, but that was brave enough to tell you to sit down or shut up or that you're wrong. Or that you're acting stubborn."

"An alpha," I mused. The movie 300 instantly popped to mind. There was some serious testosterone in that movie.

I reached for the television control, wondering if it was too late to change our viewing choice for the evening, but Addison, reading my mind, snatched the control away. "Focus. You definitely need an alpha," she agreed, sipping her wine before standing and walking back towards the kitchen for the bottle, carrying the control with her. She brought both the bottle and the control back to the living room and topped off my glass before refilling her own and sitting back on the couch, setting the control on my coffee table. The table was incredibly old with water stains all over its surface. "And it certainly sounds like they both have it in them to be just that."

"So what do I do?"

She shrugged. "Wait and see. If your gut isn't already screaming with one decision or another, then take your time. If they're not rushing you to make a decision — and they shouldn't — do what's right for you. Now, let's watch a movie. 300?"

As the movie ended with the familiar swell of emotions and a fadeout to the credits, I stretched my arms high above my head. "What time is it?" I asked, looking around for a clock.

Addison reached for her cell. "About 1:30. We should probably get to bed. I have to work in the morning."

"Couch or bed?" I asked, standing.

"You kidding? Now that I know your sheets aren't filthy, I can't wait to snuggle with you." She grinned and took my wine glass, carrying it into the kitchen, along with our long empty wine bottle.

"Meet me in there," I teased, sashaying away.

"Em?" she called just after I'd stepped into the bedroom.

"Yeah?" I hollered back, straightening my sheets and fluffing pillows.

"Your phone is ringing."

I cursed under my breath. It was probably work, asking me to come photograph a crime scene. Nothing good came of any activity that happened after midnight. I didn't understand why people couldn't get that through their thick, partying skulls. I shuffled back towards the kitchen and heard Addison's hushed voice as she answered on my behalf. Shooting her a dirty look, I fought the urge to shake my fist at her. Now I'd have to go in for sure. At least if I hadn't answered, they'd just assume I was asleep. Now I'd have to explain that the real reason I couldn't come in and photograph dead bodies was because I'd been drinking, an excuse that always failed to amuse the department.

As soon as I shuffled into the kitchen, Addison walked quickly towards me. "Just a second. She's right here," she told the person on the other end of the line.

"Why did you answer?" I hissed as she covered the speaker with her free hand. "I'm sloshed. I can't possibly go into work right now."

"It's not work," she said, thrusting the phone towards me again. "The caller ID said it was your mother."

"Ma?" I asked Addison, confused, snatching away the phone. "Why is she calling this late?" I felt a cold fear rise up from my belly and clutch my heart tightly in its grip. Something told me I didn't want to know the answer, but it was impossible to call back the words.

"It's Riley," Addison answered gravely.

"My niece?"

Addison nodded. "She was kidnapped."

Needless to say there wasn't much in terms of information that I was able to pull out of my mother on that phone call. Even my usually level-headed father was having difficulty providing details — not that there were many.

Earlier that evening, Riley had been grounded. She was a pretty ornery kid and got grounded on a fairly regular basis. However, she also had a tendency to sneak out of her bedroom window and over to my parents' house just down the street when she got sick of being cooped up in her room. Suffice to say that when my sister-in-law, Rachel, went upstairs to collect Riley for dinner and her daughter was missing, Rachel wasn't exactly worried. Fast forward 30 minutes: a brisk walk to my parents' house and a search of their property with no Riley turning up, well, you've probably never seen panic quite like it. And in case you didn't know, panic in a small town travels really, really fast. It's a virus that can't be stopped until everyone has been infected.

My dad, retired from the police force, took charge immediately. Within a short span of time, his buddies, both those retired and those still on the force, had convened at my parents' house and formulated a plan. Pop had just about everyone in town searching for his granddaughter.

When no one could find her in a reasonable amount of time, my parents decided to call me and fill me in, begging me to come home and be with the family during their time of need. They needn't have even asked, but that's how we Midwesterners are — afraid to inconvenience someone.

The drive to my hometown is boring, but fast. I was already packing a duffle bag before I'd ended the call. My mother was insisting that I waited until morning before I started driving. While normally I would have protested, the bottle of wine I'd participated in drinking was telling me otherwise. Waiting a few hours would be safer. I'd be distracted enough on the drive without adding alcohol to things, even if it had been over an hour since my last drink.

After my mom and I had hung up, I turned to Addison. Suddenly, a terrible thought descended upon me and I felt my stomach lurch. My hands grew clammy as I gripped my phone and turned it over and over in my hands. "Do you think- do you think Barry could have-"

"No," Addison soothed, rushing to my side and hugging my shoulders. She quickly moved the duffle bag, which was splayed open on my bed, and sat us both down. "He's in prison. There's no way he participated in any of this." She smoothed back a piece of hair that had fallen into my eyes. "How do they know for sure that she was kidnapped?"

"There was a ransom note," I confessed. "They found it on the floor just under her bed. It must have fallen from the dresser or something. It's why at first Rachel thought

Riley had maybe just gone over to be with my parents. She didn't even see it."

Addison hesitated before asking her next question. "Just to play devil's advocate, are we sure that Riley didn't write the note herself? The town is pretty small. If no one saw anything, I'd be surprised if Riley was really kidnapped. Was the note made of magazine clippings or typed on a computer or anything like that?" Addison and I had grown up neighbors. If anyone knew what tragedy was like in a small town, she did. Her imagination was running wild with an exposé — I could feel it.

"So they say," I sighed. "It sounds like it was typed on a computer. Demanding money."

"How much?"

"I didn't ask."

"That'll be something we want to find out as soon as possible. The drop date, too," Addison mused.

"The what?"

"The date they demand collection. It's usually some ridiculous time frame."

"Are you still going to stay the night?"

"Of course," she answered. "Unless you need to be alone. I'd completely understand."

"Please stay."

"I will. But only if you promise to take me by my place in the morning for an overnight bag. I'm coming with you."

I hugged her tightly. "You're such a good friend," I whispered.

Before Addison and I fell asleep that night, we each made a few calls. She to her boss, pitching Riley's kidnapping as a human interest piece. Thankfully, the news never sleeps and he was not only wide awake at two in the morning, but also agreed to let her write it, securing her visit with my family for as long as it could take.

With the media at our disposal, Addison and I were bound to generate some leads. While most of them would probably be false, you only needed one or two that were legitimate before you were on your way to solving the case. After Addie had hung up with her editor, she called Rory and explained the situation. He kindly offered to pack a bag based on the odds and ends she had at his apartment and drop it off, so that we could leave straight from my apartment in the morning. "He even offered to put my delicates through the laundry so that I'd have clean panties," she told me smugly. If I'd at all doubted Rory's dedication to Addison before, it was now secured.

Meanwhile, I called my own contacts that made their lives this line of work: James, Mika and my good friend Janet, who now resided in Tampa, where her husband, Rob, had gotten transferred for work. I also left a message for Carly Ipson, Barry's old partner. While he'd been crooked as a Halloween broomstick, Janet had once sworn to me that Carly was as good as they got in the Milwaukee PD. Unfortunately, Carly had been on vacation during the whole Barry trying to kill me thing, so we hadn't actually had an opportunity to work together yet. As her specialty wasn't homicide, we didn't exactly have a reason to run into one another on the job. Still, Janet's word was good enough for me. I figured it couldn't hurt to include Carly, even if it turned out that she wasn't interested in helping.

James and Mika, who had both picked up their phones, each insisted on joining Addison and I in the morning. While I had no doubt that both of them could be utilized in the search, I was hesitant to have them with me in the same place at the same time for goodness knew how long. It had the potential to be disastrous at an already highly emotional time. Yet, I also found that I couldn't say "no" to either of them.

Janet had also answered my late night distress call, despite the fact that it was a full hour later in Florida. "Em?" she asked. "What's wrong?" In one long, shuddery breath, I explained everything. When I'd finished, there was a brief moment of silence. Next, I heard the low quiet mumbling of a man I assumed to be Rob, the shuffling of blankets and the clicking of a keyboard. "Looks like there's a 6:30am direct to Milwaukee International from Tampa. I'll rent a car there and meet you at your parents' place this afternoon. What's the name of your hometown, again?"

I gave her directions and thanked her profusely. While I realized that I'd secretly hoped she'd be able to make it back, if only to support me, I didn't think she would actually do it. The cost a flight taking off in less than 12 hours was likely astronomical and while it was well within her budget, it was far from expected. "This is really above and beyond," I said gratefully.

"You'd do the same for me." I could hear her smile as she said it.

Once our calls were made, Addison and I waited up until Rory stopped by. In addition to Addie's bag, he brought us each a pint of Ben & Jerry's. We wrapped him in a huge group hug. When we finally pulled away, he shrugged sheepishly. "It's the least I could do." Promising to hold down the fort at *Food Porn* while we were out, he ducked into the stairwell with a wave goodbye. "Call me if you need anything. I'll get it to you," he promised.

Neither Addison nor I slept well. Sometime before sunrise, we rolled out of bed, showered and headed to my car, which was parked in the lot out back. James and Mika were both there, too, staring one another down. I realized that I hadn't told either of them that the other would also be coming, but hopefully they'd forgive me, given the circumstances. When they heard Addison and I approaching, they each pushed themselves off of their respective vehicles, which they'd been leaning on. James's was a large black truck, while Mika drove a slightly rusted, outdated Jeep. "You guys should have waited in the lobby," I insisted. "It's too cold to be standing outside."

"Didn't want to bother you," Mika assured me, coming over to take my bag. Not to be outdone, James made a grab for Addison's.

"Thanks," she whispered through her scarf, her hot breath creating a soft cloud that quickly dissipated. Additionally, I'd been correct about her boots. They were high heeled and seemed to have a pair of leg warmers sewn to them. I briefly wondered where she found such things.

Tossing the overnight bags into the back of my Suburban — a gift from Rory after my last car blew up — both men turned to look at me. "Together or-" James began.

"Separate," I cut him off. He looked momentarily wounded and so I added, "we need all of the vehicles out there searching that we can get."

They both seemed to accept this and hopped back into their Sport Utility Vehicles, revving the engines back to life. Once my own car had, had a few moments to warm up, I backed out of my parking spot and turned towards the interstate. "Coffee?" Addison asked, pleadingly.

Nodding, I pulled into a coffee drive-thru, which was conveniently serving breakfast, as well. One muffin, two breakfast burritos and two large coffees later, we pulled off to the side while Mika and James retrieved their orders. Once everyone was settled, we were back on the highway, headed northwest. I called the home phone to let my parents know that we were on our way. When they didn't answer, I left a message, figuring that they were either passed out from exhaustion, or out searching for Riley. Either way, neither answered their cell phone frequently enough to resort to a follow-up call using that method.

About two hours later, I slowly crept my car up the block

that my parents lived on. It was still an early hour, but their brownstone was buzzing with activity. The closest parking I could find was nearly a block over. It seemed like the entire town was involved in the search for my missing niece, not that I was surprised. Actually, given the size of the population and how well-known my dad was, the whole town probably WAS involved in the search. People in bright orange vests gathered in small groups across the lawn. Some were holding maps. Some were holding radios. About half of them gripped a cup of coffee and looked rather disheveled, as though they'd been out all night. I surmised that this was the official "shift change."

As I approached the house with my duffle, Addison hot on my heels, I heard a voice boom. "Is that little Marian Moyer?"

I turned and saw my dad's best friend and old partner standing amid a group of uniforms. "Frank!" I cried happily, dropping my duffle and launching myself into his big-barreled chest. "I didn't know you were here."

"Where else would I be?" he asked loudly, taking my arms and pulling me away from him. "Let me have a quick look at you!" His gray eyes sparkled as he turned me around in a circle. Suddenly, he caught sight of Addison. "Addie Mae!" he cried enthusiastically, pulling her in for a quick hug. After a few seconds, he took our hands and looked at us solemnly. "I'm so sorry that these are the circumstances I get to see you girls in. I'd best get back to work. Marian, your family is in the kitchen."

Giving him a sad smile, I squeezed his hand before turning to pick up my duffle, and walked towards the front door. James and Mika stood, sunglasses on, arms crossed on the front porch. They'd pass for my security detail, had they not been dressed down in jeans and ball caps.

Squeezing through them, I opened the front door and was immediately gripped by the smells of burnt coffee grounds and bacon grease. I was home. "Ma?" I called, setting my bag just off of the entryway. "We're here."

"We?" I heard her ask, as she slid back her kitchen chair and padded across the vinyl. I loved my parents' house. I'd grown up here and, even though most of the floorings and furniture were outdated, it was a place of peace and comfort. The storm that was whirling just beyond their windows on the front lawn may as well have not even been happening. The atmosphere inside was calm and hopeful, filled with love and terrible tasting food. As my mother rounded the corner into the hall, she took in Addison, as well as James and Mika, the latter of whom she'd never met. She'd met James once, long ago when she'd come to visit me in college and we'd ran into him in the student union. I couldn't be sure she remembered him. At any rate, he'd definitely changed. My niece may be priority number one, but two attractive men that are my age, accompanying me to my mother's house, was a very, very close second. She'd be making time for questions.

As we passed one another in the hallway, she gently squeezed my arm and gave me a look as if to say "hubba

hubba." I had to agree. "Welcome!" she said, enveloping Addie in a quick hug. My mother is a rounder, classily dressed middle-aged woman with wild gray streaks in her dark brown hair. She wears her black cat eye glasses on a silver chain around her neck and speaks with a thick Boston accent, usually as she's pointing at you with her long, lacquered nails or cooking something completely inedible. My father isn't shy about admitting that he didn't marry my mother for her culinary expertise. "Addison, I knew you were coming, but I'm not sure I've ever met these gentlemen before." She pulled away from Addie and held out her hand so that she could properly meet James and Mika. Once the pleasantries were out of the way, me failing to remind her that James had been my college crush, I took my mother's elbow and began to guide her towards the kitchen. "James and Mika are friends of ours and work as private investigators. They thought that they might be able to help find Riley. That's why they've come along."

"Who's a private investigator?" I heard my dad holler. I was pretty sure that he and most of his buddies had probably never worked with PIs before. There wasn't much of a need out here. In fact, before Riley's kidnapping, the last sensational case that had required out-of-state police had taken place over 60 years prior. For the first time, I found myself worrying if everyone would mesh well. It's a well-known fact among law enforcement that cops don't like fancy PIs coming in, taking over their cases.

If James and Mika had been called for their expertise personally by the local PD, that would have been a different story.

"Pop, I'd like you to meet James and Mika," I said nervously as we rounded the corner. My father sat around the rickety '70s kitchen table, along with my brother, John, and my sister-in-law, Rachel. A large plate of sad, blackened bacon sat almost untouched in the middle of the table. A few breadcrumbs were left on a serving platter that had obviously contained toast at some point — the one thing that my mother never seemed to screw up. There were also four coffee mugs in various stages of fullness. "They are both private investigators in Milwaukee and good friends of mine. They've offered to help us find Riley and I don't think we're in a position to be turning down help."

Rachel, a beautiful blond-haired, green-eyed woman with milky white skin, gawked at my suitors. After a few seconds, she snapped her jaw shut and dropped her chin, toying with the food that still sat on her plate. Both men seemed to give women that reaction. My poor brother looked like he hadn't showered in days. His floppy auburn hair flipped over his small hazel eyes, while he glumly propped up his chin in his hand. The bags under his eyes were dark and protruding. A smattering of freckles spilled across his hands and arms, eventually disappearing under his t-shirt, which was olive green and covered in old stains.

My father, in whom you could still find handsomeness,

stared at us suspiciously from his kitchen chair. He still had a full head of hair, though it had gone gray over the years. He was a larger man, still slightly brown from a summer spent outside doing yard work in the short shorts and cutoff shirt he always insisted on wearing to avoid the dreaded farmers tan. "I recognize you," he said, squinting at Mika and shaking his head as though it would help him clear the cobwebs and recall. "We've met before."

Mika looked like he was thinking hard for a few moments, but shook his head. "I don't think we have, sir. I'm-"

"Naked!" My father cried suddenly, pushing back his chair. He stood and began to wag his finger towards Mika. "You! You were naked! In my daughter's magazine last month. I saw it! I saw the issue at the Penny Post!"

"Oh, no," I muttered under my breath. The Penny Post was a local grocery store. Mika had not, in fact, been totally naked. My subjects never are. However, my father never seemed to see it that way. Shirtless was naked. Shoeless was naked. Underwear only was especially naked. This coming from a reformed hippie.

Rachel's interest in the handsome strangers seemed to have returned with my dad's words. She and my brother had married just out of high school. While they seemed wildly in love, I couldn't blame her for being curious. I would have been.

"I was doing some undercover work-" Mika began.

My father cut him off. "I'll tell you what covers you can't

be under! My daughter's!" my father roared.

Mika took a small step backwards. "I only meant-"

"Can we focus?" I cut in sharply, staring down my father. "He has gotten nowhere near my covers."

"Not from lack of trying, probably," James muttered.

Mika's face grew dark and, for a moment, I thought he was going to punch James in the face. I'll admit that the idea of this wasn't as entirely perplexing as it should have been.

"Okay!" Addison said brightly. "Let's all just take a minute, shall we? Take some deep breaths? Talk it out. Marian and I will be right back." Taking me by the elbow, she led me down the hall to my old bedroom and shut the door behind us. I crossed to my window and peeked through the blinds, bewildered by the amount of activity outside. I heard Addison take a deep breath behind me, before she set into one of her Lamaze episodes. In addition to her ease of panic, Addie has a wicked temper. A while back, her therapist suggested some deep breathing exercises. Addie had taken the advice to the extreme. However crazy she sounded when she did it, I had to say, it was working for her. I hadn't been privy to an explosion in over a month. The episode that had just gone down in the kitchen was usually enough to set her off. Old Addison would have leapt into the fray in an effort to protect me. New Addison helped me escape.

A few seconds later, once her heavy breaths had ceased, Addison strode across the floor and joined me at my window. She peeked out at all the activity, as well. "You sure you can handle all of this?" she asked me. "Your dad? James? Mika?"

I shrugged. "What choice do I have? It's family."

She nodded and we stood in silence for a moment, not knowing what to say to one another. Finally, Addison giggled. "Your dad really is a trip."

I rolled my eyes. "Tell me about it. Let's get this show on the road."

We emerged from my room and headed back towards the kitchen, where Dad was filling James and Mika in on the details of my niece's disappearance. "$62,300," he was saying.

"What about $62,300?" Addison asked him. "Is that the ransom?" I could see the wheels in her head turn as she began drafting the first round of her human interest piece. The ransom amount. The desperation a small, poor, factory town felt over the imposed timeline of coming up with the cash. Addison would have the whole state cheering for Riley's return in no time.

"Yes," my dad responded, gravely. "No due date. No exchange location. Just a number and instructions that we should wait for more instructions. What kind of an idiot operation is that?"

Quiet descended as everyone contemplated that for a second. "Weird number," Mika finally commented. On that, at least, we could all agree.

As it turned out, about 800 people from the town were split into three shifts, searching for Riley. People were scanning every field, farmhouse and playground. Thus far, there was nothing to go on. There were no signs of forced entry into John and Rachel's small ranch-style home, but just about everyone around here slept with their doors and windows unlocked. It was just what you did in a town this size. Riley's room hadn't revealed any suspicious fingerprints, from what the police were able to tell. Crime scene investigators had come all the way from Green Bay as a favor to Frank and my dad. My niece hadn't been missing long enough for a missing person's report to be filed, but by being on the force, my dad had a few tricks up his sleeve. "We're going to keep looking until we find her," my father assured all of us. "I won't leave a single stone unturned."

My family had been awake since they first discovered that Riley was missing. Fueled by nothing more than coffee and adrenaline, their bodies were beginning to wear out around lunch time. I shooed my parents off to bed, promising to wake them if there was any news. My brother and Rachel slunk down to his old bedroom, just across the hall from mine, in order to catch a little sleep. They couldn't bring themselves to return home just yet. Riley's smiling face would gleam at them from nearly every photo that hung on their walls. She was their light. Their life. Their only child.

Once they were all safely to bed, Addison, James, Mika

and I gathered around the kitchen table. I collected coffee mugs while Addison picked up plates. Even as we rinsed things out in the sink, we were trying to piece together the strange case that was my niece's disappearance. "I don't think she ran away like you suggested when Ma first called," I confessed to Addie, scrubbing at the grease that clung tightly to a plate. "She just wouldn't do it."

"She runs over here a lot," Addison supplied.

"Yes, but that's different," I told her. "She's always done that. Completely disappearing? A ransom note? That's way too elaborate for a 12 year old."

"Is it? She's in middle school," Addison answered. "Junior high kids can be sneaky."

"Yeah, but- just- not like this," I sputtered, turning off the water faucet angrily. "She'd never do this to us. Whose side are you on?"

Addison eyed me hard. "Yours," she answered. "But I can't have you thinking like an aunt. I need you thinking like you're photographing a crime scene. I need you to see things that others don't see. If you can't, you're no good to this investigation and you need to step off and let the rest of us handle it." She paused and her gaze softened. "Do you think we can get into her bedroom? Or will it be secured?"

"There are ways," James said from the kitchen table. I jumped and turned, having forgotten that he and Mika were there.

Mika was chewing his lip, gazing off into nothing. After a

moment, he said, "I'm still bothered by the ransom. That really is a weird amount of money. Why not $60,000? Why not $65,000? Hell, why not $100,000?"

"Think there's a connection?" James asked him.

Mika shrugged. "Not sure, but worth looking into financial records and seeing what we can find."

"Wait, what?" I asked, drying my hands on a dish rag. "Whose financial records? Why are you looking into them?"

"We need to see if your brother and sister-in-law have any debts," James told me. "If there are any amounts owed that are similar to the amount being asked for ransom, we may have a lead."

I shook my head. "John and Rachel have always had plenty of money."

"What do they do for a living?" Mika asked.

"She's a waitress and he works over at the post office." Mika and James eyed one another. I placed my hands on my hips and felt my nostrils flaring in defiance. "Look at where they live," I hissed quietly, gesturing around. "This isn't exactly SoHo. It's not like they need to run a company to make ends meet." When both men continued to look unsure, I added, "Plus, I'm pretty sure they can still ask my parents for help if they need it that badly."

"What if they didn't want to ask for help?"

I snorted and looked to Addison for backup. My brother owned a house, worked hard for a living, had a few nice things and took good care of his family. However, my parents had never fully cut him off. I assume it's because he and Rachel had Riley when they were still teenagers. My parents still viewed both of them as kids, forever locked in a teenage time warp. This despite the fact that Riley herself was almost a teenager. They wanted for nothing. They always would. Addison knew this. She'd never defend such a preposterous idea.

Addison looked at me and shrugged. "Maybe not a terrible idea to just look. Just in case."

"Fine," I muttered. I hated the idea of anyone thinking that my brother had secrets to hide. While he and I hadn't been super close growing up, we'd come to love and respect one another over the last few years. He was a good man. An honest one. Surely he would have mentioned troubles of any kind to someone by now if it meant his daughter's life. Right?

Once we'd agreed on an immediate plan of action, James went out to speak with the police that were gathered on the front lawn. Were I being truthful, I didn't want to believe that my brother or his wife were capable of getting into trouble to the point that my beloved niece would become a target. John was so good-natured, trusting and a wonderful provider for his girls. Rachel wasn't the brightest crayon in the box, but she was beautiful and sweet and loved her little family dearly. Surely neither would jeopardize things.

Addison and I carried our things down to my old bedroom. After adding a few more layers to our fairly light, comfortable driving attire, we went outside to join the fray. No sooner had I stepped off my porch than my phone began to ring. Checking the caller ID, I answered quickly. "Land safely?"

"Yup," Janet answered. "I'm headed over to pick up my rental. I'll see you in a few hours."

I rattled off the address one last time and hung up, feeling slightly more relaxed. Janet was about five years older than me with a motherly quality I'd always coveted. She propped me up in life in a way that no one else could simply by being herself. Janet was one of those amazing full-of-life individuals that you only came across once, maybe twice in your lifetime. She and I met at a holiday party for the department several years ago. I'd forced myself to go to the soiree, having nothing better to do on a Friday night. I'd been standing in a corner, awkwardly drinking my alcohol-free punch when she convinced me to join her in the middle of the room. I'm not sure how she did it, but she did. As soon as the music began to quiet and before the DJ could pick a new tune, Janet had simultaneously started a holiday choir and "the wave" among several officers that were known for being a surly lot, choosing me as her partner in crime. We'd been friends ever since.

I find it incredibly disappointing that she and her husband have opted not to have children — I think she'd be an amazing mom. Still, she makes one hell of a cop and I was honored that she'd be joining our ragtag group of misfits as both a sounding board and an additional brain.

The cold had begun to nip at my cheeks. Graying, slushy snow was everywhere and the wind was increasingly brutal. James walked over to Addison and I, as Mika continued speaking with Frank. "I think we're going to need to hack John's financials," he sighed, tucking a small notebook into his coat pocket.

"Hack them?" I asked, confused. "Why? Like on a computer? Can you do that?"

James smiled quickly. "I can do just about anything, Kitten."

I felt a blush immediately rise to my cheeks. I adored that nickname he'd given me. We'd been at the pet store, buying Fred more food, when I'd paused to look through the adoptable animals. One particular brown and white tabby has caught my attention and James had teased me about it all the way home. Willing my bright red cheeks to go away, I suddenly became rather interested in my shoes.

"How can we help?" Addison piped up, tightening the scarf around her nose and mouth. She fumbled slightly – her mittens were thick and fashionable, though not functional in the slightest. I watched her struggle for a few seconds, bemused. James eventually pulled off his own gloves and assisted. "Thanks," she muttered quietly.

"Welcome," he answered. Then, to both of us, "I think that the two of you should help with the search efforts for a while. Get a feel for how they're searching for Riley and if there seem to be any holes in how the search is being handled. Mika and I are going to set up camp in the kitchen. We're more useful trying to figure this mess out by using our brains instead of our braun."

"We have brains, too," I joked. He nodded but didn't crack a smile, so I rushed ahead. "That all makes sense. I'll just go get assignments from Frank."

"Marian, wait," James said, grabbing my arm. When I turned, I could see his beautiful, green eyes filled with something I'd never seen before. I swallowed, knowing that I wouldn't like what he was about to say. "I just need you to know that no matter what we find or how we use the information- it isn't meant to hurt you or your family."

We stared at one another for a long moment. Finally, I nodded. Pulling away, I began trekking towards Frank. In other words, James was saying that he and Mika would be treating suspects in this case no differently than a run-of-the-mill average Joe they'd cracked down on hundreds of times. If my brother or his beautiful wife had anything to do with Riley's disappearance, they were screwed.

Thirty minutes later, Addison and I had driven to the far west end of town. Looping our borrowed orange security vests over layers of sweatshirts and coats, we jumped out and ran to join the other able-bodied folks. Some were searching a drainage ditch, while others were pushing through the snow-blown field with large sticks. "They're searching for a body," Addison whispered. I shuddered, thinking of my poor niece getting kidnapped, injured and then dumped, freezing to death in an empty cornfield. Shaking my head, I cleared the image from my mind. I couldn't think like that. I wouldn't.

Just like everyone else that was nearby, Addison and I took turns wading through the snow and thawing out in our truck. Wisconsin winters, especially northern Wisconsin winters, were punishing on the human body. It didn't help that the year was seeing record breaking low temperatures.

Hours later, when both the long drainage ditch and the wide open field were dubbed "clean," the group of us that had searched them headed back for home base. "Janet should be here by now," I told Addison through chattering teeth, as I glanced at the clock. Pulling out my phone, I checked for missed calls or messages. There were none. "Hopefully she's here and has made herself at home."

Once near the house, we realized we'd need to park a few blocks away again. My parents' place was still hopping with activity. I checked the clock on the dash. 2:47pm. Riley hadn't yet been missing 24 hours. Time was, fortunately, on our side for now. The unspoken rule was that you had about two days to hatch a lead before a case was in danger of running cold. I shuddered. I'd been as cold on this case as I cared to be.

Looping around the back side of the house, Addie nudged me as we passed a small silver sports car with Kansas plates. "That's got to be her," she told me. Sport Utility Vehicles rentals were hard to come by in snow country in the winter. I nodded as I nudged the Suburban into a parallel parking space. Glancing at one another, we took a deep breath, burrowed deeply into our winter wear and opened our car doors at the same time. A heavy wind blasted our faces as we scurried up the sidewalk and around the front of the house. We waved quickly to Frank, who was standing with a pile of volunteers in the garage. They were gathered amid several space heaters, which appeared to be running full blast. Tucking through the front door, we closed it behind us and immediately started removing our gear, soaked through with snow and mud from the fields.

"Marian, is that you?" someone hissed from the kitchen.

"Yeah," I hissed back.

I heard a chair push back and then footsteps padding across the kitchen floor. James peeked around the corner. "We need you in here."

"Just a second," I whispered, shaking out of my heavy winter coat.

"Now," he demanded.

My gaze snapped towards his when I heard the urgency in his voice. Something wasn't right. I struggled to kick out of my soggy boots. As quickly as I could, I slipped and slid towards the kitchen in my thick, fuzzy socks. At one point, I nearly crash landed into a wall. My mother may not be much of a cook, but she prides herself on a clean home and waxes the floors at least every other week. Addison and I used to take turns pushing each other down the length of the hallway when we were younger. Surprisingly, neither of us broke so much as a nail. "This better be good," I muttered, rounding the corner with Addison, rubbing my forehead where I'd caught myself on the wall. My outlook brightened considerably when I noticed that Janet was hovering over Mika's laptop.

"Hey, girl!" she said, coming over to swoop me into a big hug.

As tightly as I could, I hugged her back. When we finally pulled away, I gave her my sincerest smile and a squeeze on the arm. I didn't want to get mushy in front of everyone. I was afraid that if I let my guard down, even for a second, I'd become a total basket case, especially in front of her. I was incredibly grateful that she'd flown so far for a friend in need. "You meet everybody?" I asked, struggling to keep the emotion out of my voice.

She nodded. "Who is the guy out front running the show?"

"That's Frank," Addison answered.

"Old friend of my pop," I added. "They were partners back in the day."

"Ah," Janet responded, wrinkling her nose. "That would explain the third degree."

I smiled. "This is the biggest case they've had in years. Maybe ever. I'm sure Frank is being careful about who knows what. Plus he probably hopes that his guys can solve the mystery without the help of all us fancy city folks that carry reputations for piecing together these kinds of cases."

"Shouldn't matter so long as we find the girl," Janet muttered.

I shrugged. Janet wasn't from a small town herself. She'd grown up in a suburb of Chicago. It was just a different mentality that you had to come to understand out here. In a case like this, it was easy to unintentionally step on a few toes. The police wanted to appear competent and the more people I brought in from the city to help, the harder it would be to convince Frank and the others that we trusted their abilities. Still, this was my family. No one was going to tell me who I could and couldn't involve in the search. While there wasn't a way to express that to Frank, I didn't have the time nor the patience to stroke egos around here. We had a very small window of opportunity with which to locate my niece. That window was closing with each passing hour. I could only hope that Mika and James were onto something, seeing as how no one else seemed to be.

"Marian, you need to have a look at this," Mika said, swiveling his computer screen to face me.

I quickly scanned the document, but shook my head. It was a large spreadsheet which looked to be plugged with some truly dumbfounding numbers. "Are those John's accounts?" I asked, confused. "Who has that kind of money?" I paused and looked from James to Mika. "Other than you two." Both men were self-made millionaires. I'd never actually seen their bank accounts, but based off of something Barry had said to me back before I knew he was crazy, their balances were probably similar to what was on the spreadsheet before me.

"Those aren't," James answered, turning his own laptop to face me. "But these are."

Even though it felt incredibly invasive, I scanned James's screen. It was filled with modest but respectable savings and debt. I nodded my head as I continued down through the spreadsheet. "These look fine," I mumbled quietly to myself. After I few seconds I moved my gaze back towards Mika's computer and felt my brow again wrinkle in confusion. "So whose account is this?" The numbers were astronomical and not one of them was debt. James shifted uncomfortably but didn't make eye contact. Mika coughed and turned to look at Janet. Her cheeks grew red as she glanced down at her lap. "Oh, for heaven's sake," I snapped, moving my hands to my hips. "Just tell me!"

After a long pause, Janet finally met my gaze. "They're Rachel's accounts."

I felt my world sway slightly and I reached out to grab the kitchen table for support. Addison quickly snaked an arm around my waist to prop me upright, as well. "What- why- are you sure? Maybe it's another Rachel Moyer."

Mika shook his head. "We're sure."

"A lot of spouses have separate accounts," I supplied.

"Like this?" Mika asked, highlighting the last deposit on his screen. "And I don't mean this in the way it's probably going to sound but... That's a lot of money for a waitress to be making."

"Maybe she just has another job that we don't know about."

James snorted. "Like what? A call girl?"

I felt panic rise in my throat. Desperately, I turned to face Addison, hoping for reassurance. "Deep breaths," Addison whispered. Gently, she grasped my wrists and began flopping my hands around in small circles as Janet came around the table to fan my face with her notebook. "In...2...3...out...5...6..." Addie was saying.

"Stop it!" I cried, flapping her away.

"Okay, everybody just calm down," James cried, raising his hands in a peaceful gesture. Nonetheless, he was looking directly at me.

I felt myself suck in a breath. Slowly my head began to cock to one side and my eyes narrowed so significantly, I could barely see him. "Calm down?" I asked in a low voice. The air left the room as James shifted uncomfortably again, stood and shuffled a few steps back. I took a long stride towards him to close the gap. "Did you just tell me to calm down?"

"He did," Addison said, matter-of-factly.

"He should know better than to say those words to a woman," Janet added. "To any woman, really."

Mika remained planted in his chair at the kitchen table, barely moving, eyes locked on the fireworks that had been lit all around him. He, wisely, chose not to speak, even when James eyed him in desperation.

"I just meant we shouldn't be jumping to any conclusions," James stuttered. "That's all."

"Shouldn't jump to conclusions," I repeated, taking another step to close the shrinking gap between us.

"She's repeating herself," Addison whispered.

"He's in trouble," Janet agreed.

"Kitten," James began. I growled menacingly in the back of my throat. James looked pleadingly to Addison and Janet for help but they just smiled and shrugged. Mika remained glued to his chair, unmoving. I continued to stand just inches away from James, curling and uncurling my fists, debating my attack. After a few seconds, James cleared his throat. "It might not be what we think," he said quietly, taking my furled fists gently in his hands and guiding me back to my chair.

I paused, blinking at this realization. Suddenly, my brain kicked into gear. "You're sure that John isn't listed on a single one of those accounts?" I asked no one in particular.

Mika shook his head. "Just Rachel. Trust me. We've searched every possible way."

"I suggested that already," Janet said quietly from behind me. "That we look for individual accounts. A case I solved a while back gave me the idea. We looked at your parents, too. When there was nothing out of sorts there, I just threw out the idea of Rachel having her own set up."

"Why didn't someone report it?" I asked incredulously, pouring over the numbers again. "Surely the local bank knew. No one keeps a secret around here." Agnes Thorton was the lead banker at the only bank within about 30 miles. She was older, angry and had a tendency to report on the financial successes and failures of local townsfolk over small talk at the local meat market. It wasn't legal, but a small town like this ran by a different set of rules.

"It's a big name bank in the city," Mika supplied. "She's not using the mom and pop shop around the corner like the rest of your family. She's using an outfit that has been known to partake in some pretty shady business."

"Why has no one shut them down, then?" I asked,

distressed. "If people know that the bank she's using is crooked, surely something can be done about it. She can't be the first person to use it."

"No one can prove it yet," Mika responded with a shrug. "FBI has been on it for a few years. Gathering a case and everything. It's a fact known among mob bosses that the bank caters-"

I cut James off with an aghast "mob bosses?"

"We're talking the underbelly of society here, Sugar," Mika told me, standing and coming around the table. James stepped aside so that Mika could squat down in front of me and take my hands in his. I suddenly felt so small and lost, as I searched his eyes for signs of joking. There were none. "Some major criminal players. Killers for hire. Drug cartel. Mob bosses. Money launderers. You name it, they have probably held an account there at one time or another."

"But they wire it all to the Cayman Islands just before the FBI can close a case on them," James said. "Then they disappear for ten years. Don't ask me how they manage it, I only know that they do. Everyone is suddenly Frank Abagnale."

"Sometimes they return under an entirely new identity and get away with it all over again until the government catches on," Mika added.

It was all too much. I felt myself sway in my chair as the room around me blurred and spun. At some point, I felt Addison massaging my shoulders as Janet handed me a cold glass of water. I gulped it greedily. "So why would Rachel have- I mean, you don't think that she-" My mouth grew dry again. My words weren't making sense — in my mouth or in my head. Suddenly our earlier conversation dawned on me. I whirled around and grabbed Mika's computer. Reading through Rachel's accounts again, I began shaking with excitement. "Wait," I said, pointing to the screen eagerly. "They're all positive. She doesn't owe a thing." I turned to James and Mika. "And if she did, she has plenty of money to cover it. Nothing in here suggests she owes that bizarre ransom amount." I thrust the laptop at him, hopeful.

Gently, Mika took it from my hands and set it back on the table. "That's true," he said. "But it still doesn't explain where all of her money came from. Or why she's holding it at a bank with a bad reputation. These are the questions that we need answered. They could lead us to your niece."

"We were looking for one thing but stumbled onto something much larger," Janet added. "Happens all the time."

"Maybe Rachel just doesn't know about the bank's reputation," I supplied. That didn't sound plausible, though. Even as I said it, the suggestion felt stupid. Of course she was aware of the bank's reputation. It was over a three-hour drive from where she lived. She'd picked that bank. Had chosen it specifically because it could offer the cover that she needed.

"Even if that's true," James said, "how does a waitress

put away over three million dollars?"

"And if it was legitimate, why wouldn't she deposit local?" Janet added. "For that matter, why not invest it in stocks and bonds and things that make sense, instead of collecting on some crappy low interest rate? Set some aside for Riley's college fund?"

My heart ached at the mention of my niece. "You're wrong," I said, stubbornly, feeling the lie slip easily from my lips. "Rachel can't have had anything to do with this."

"Thank you, Marian," said a frosty voice behind us. Slowly, we turned to see Rachel standing, arms crossed, in the entrance to the kitchen.

The room suddenly felt significantly smaller than it had a few moments ago. I grew red with embarrassment, knowing full well that I'd defended her because she was family, not because I was sure of her innocence.

Rachel took a moment to glare at everyone but me, her body language defiant. Her beautiful blond hair spilled in flat sheets over her shoulders, her bright eyes narrowed in accusation. She was slightly skinnier than was probably healthy, but perhaps it was the strain of the situation. Then again, she'd never seemed quite so tiny and bird-like before. My imagination was running away with itself, imagining her on drugs of every kind that were quietly speeding up her metabolism, wasting her away to almost nothing. I shook my head to clear it.

The hairs on the back of my neck stood on end as Rachel continued to scan my small crew, gathered tightly in the kitchen. For as long as I'd known her, which was over ten years, Rachel had always come across as your typical, gorgeous dumb blond. Cunning and deceitful had never actually crossed my mind as words to describe her. Still, standing there was an entirely different person than I had come to know. I found myself wondering if this was a side of her that my brother was familiar with. I'd have to ask him when no one else was nearby.

"Tell me, Rachel," James said slowly, breaking the silence, "why do you feel the need to hide over three million dollars in a secret bank account?" His hands were pushed deep into his pockets and he rocked back on his heels, staring her down curiously.

"I should have you arrested," Rachel growled. "All of you." She turned to look down the hallway to make sure that no one else was awake and ready to join our conversation. I felt myself shrink back slightly at her anger. Being a rather passive-aggressive person myself when it came to unhinged emotion, I tended to avoid conflicts whenever possible. I could see that this wouldn't be one of those instances. The only solution was to make myself small — very, very small.

James held out his wrists as though he were awaiting handcuffs and smiled. Rachel continued to level him with a glare. "I'm waiting, Peach," he told her with a wink. "Silver is one of my better colors. Try not to make them too tight, though. I have sensitive wrists."

Huffing, Rachel stepped past James and into the kitchen. "Why are you hacking into my bank accounts?" she asked Mika. James smiled to himself and turned, offering me a wink. I was frozen in place, unsure of how I could defuse tensions before they crept any higher.

"We were looking into Riley's kidnapping," Mika began.

"And you thought you'd find her whereabouts in my savings account?"

"We thought," Mika said patiently, "that if she'd been kidnapped as a bargaining chip for a debt you or your family owed, that it would be faster to find it in your financials than it would be to pry it out of you. Especially if the activity that you owed for was illegal," he finished, lingering on the last word a moment too long.

Rachel fixed him with a look but said nothing. I swallowed so hard that I could hear the gulp in my ears. My brain was still frozen — my body watching, waiting to see what would happen next.

"So where did it come from?" Addison asked. She was adding to her story. It was going to be another award nominee, I could tell from the edge in her voice. I was torn between getting answers and smoothing over everyone's feelings and egos. So torn, in fact, that I was totally unsure of which to do first. I continued to stare dumbly as the conversation unfolded before me.

"That's none of your business," Rachel snapped, whirling towards Addison, who smirked. Rachel was losing her cool and everyone knew it. Losing your cool was the first step towards slipping up.

"Oh, but it is," Janet told her, stepping close. Her hair was pulled back in a tight, sensible bun. Her entire demeanor echoed calmness and total control. I tried to channel her energy by closing my eyes and inhaling a few deep breaths. "Something is telling me that your hidden account is crucial to the case," Janet continued, "and we just want to know why. That's all."

Without warning, Rachel's face crumpled and she began to cry. My heart ached for her, but as I reached out to take her hand, Addison stepped in front of me. "Save it," she snapped at Rachel, whose tears ended as abruptly as they'd begun.

"Fine," Rachel hissed.

"What just happened?" I asked, confused, but no one was listening to me. They were waiting for Rachel to make her next move. It was a game of chess and I'd never learned how to play. Or perhaps, as Addison had mentioned earlier, I was simply too close to the situation.

Despite the charade of tears, Rachel didn't seem to be baiting herself any further. In fact, she just seemed to grow more and more closed off towards us. Taking a moment, she stepped around James and went to peek down the hallway, needing to confirm that we were her only captive audience. It worried me to think that she was hiding a piece of herself from my family. How had we missed it all of these years? Finally satisfied, she took a deep breath and turned to look me straight in the eyes. "What if all of that money does have something to do with the case, but I can't tell you what it is?"

My stomach dropped into my butt and I contemplated throwing up. She couldn't be serious. "Why can't you tell us?" I asked, my voice louder and more shrill than I'd intended. At a young age, my brother had nicknamed me The Teapot. Whenever I lost my cool, my voice would raise several octaves, devastating the eardrums of my offender.

Everyone in the room tensed, their faces scrunching in pain, then turned and shushed me. I felt my hands ball into rigid fists but I kept them both locked to my sides, my mouth clamped shut. I'd never punched anyone, but I had a feeling that the milestone was fast approaching if my sister-in-law was to blame after all. John would be devastated and my parents, well, they could very well die from the shock.

"Can't tell us what?" Addison encouraged, nearly leaping across the room to take Rachel by the shoulders. She gave her a slight shake and Rachel's head bobbed around like a rag doll's.

Rachel wrenched herself free of Addison's grip with a grunt, then sighed and backed up to check the hallway again. Satisfied that still no one was coming, she turned back to us. "Look, I- I can't. I can't tell you." Addison narrowed her eyes and stared at Rachel as if she'd sprouted an extra head. Rachel lowered her voice to a whisper. "I can't trust anyone."

"You can trust us," Mika said encouragingly. "We've been in this business a long time. Seen a lot of things."

Rachel just shook her head. "No," she said quietly, looking to the floor. "I can't. Really."

"A hint then?" I questioned, though still an octave too high. While everyone tensed at the tone of my voice, no one made a move to quiet me. Rather, they awaited Rachel's response with heavily baited breath.

Rachel looked up and stared at me sadly. I could tell she

was desperate to make a confession, but she wasn't sure if she should. I'm not sure how long we stood like that, acknowledging one another. Suddenly, her face lit up as if she'd thought of something. "You read books," she said to Addison, who nodded. "And sometimes, books aren't always what they seem, are they?"

"What the hell does that mean?" James asked. He was gorgeous and intelligent, but he'd never struck me as the bookish type. I imagined, instead, that his dark oak bookshelves were probably lined with an array of manly movies, several scattered awards and a few dusty candles that his mother had sent him for decorating, but that he'd never lit. Granted I'd never even so much as seen the neighborhood he lived in, let alone his house — or perhaps an apartment? We hadn't discussed it. I'd need to ask him.

"You're seriously giving us clues in riddles?" Addison asked dryly, snapping me back to the present.

"No," Rachel said. "No clues. I was just making conversation."

Janet fixed her with a glare but Rachel's facial expression didn't change. She wasn't going to budge. "We don't have time for casual conversation," I snapped, throwing my hands in the air. I could feel my breath quicken, my voice once again growing higher and higher with each word that flew from my mouth. "None of us appreciate the games. Since when does your daughter's life mean so little to you?" Rachel gasped and raised a hand to her cheek like she'd just been slapped. My palm quickly covered my mouth and my eyes grew wide. "Oh, Rachel. I'm so sorry. That was- I didn't mean to- I wasn't thinking when I said that. I know you love Riley."

After a brief stare down, Rachel lowered her hand but continued to look wounded. "We're all allowed our opinions."

"Oh, don't even try to make her feel bad," Addison seethed, bristling. "You're clearly the one that got all of us involved in this mess." She made a circular motion with her finger. "Turn that blame right on back around, sister, and take a long hard look in your compact. In fact," she began to dig around in her purse, which was hanging casually from its strap on a kitchen chair, "borrow mine." She tossed the green makeup case at Rachel, who caught it just before it hit her square in the forehead.

"Really-" I started, but Addison snapped up her hand in a "stop talking" motion. "Save it," she whispered. "I know you mean well, but you've got to stop talking right now."

I clamped my mouth shut and looked at James, who shrugged and smiled sympathetically.

"Did you know that Mr. Gregson recently lost his wife?" Rachel asked, fiddling with the green makeup compact. She opened the lid and examined her face in the small, dusty mirror before clasping it shut and tossing it back to Addison.

"What?" I cried. "What the hell does that-"

"Greg Gregson?" Addison asked, cutting me off and placing the compact back in her purse.

"Yeah," Rachel answered.

"I didn't know Grace died."

"A few months ago."

"That's terrible. I'll have to pay Mr. Gregson a visit."

"You should," Rachel said with quiet determination. "I'm sure he'd like that."

Something passed then between the two women. I caught a near undetectable nod from Addison and narrowed my eyes. She was reading between the lines. I was still catching up. I turned to the rest of our group to see if they'd noticed anything. They all appeared to be just as confused as I was by Rachel's elusiveness. I decided to try a different angle to play catch up. "Does my brother know how much you're really worth?" I asked, trying hard to keep my voice as level as possible.

Rachel's mouth twitched slightly. I could feel her sizing me up, wondering where my line of questions would lead. "He was going to. Now, I hope he never will." With that, she turned and scurried away, head down, shoulders hunched.

Once she was out of earshot, I turned from Addison to the others, and back to Addison, confused. I decided to ask the one question that was clearly on all of our minds. "What was it that you got out of her that the rest of us didn't?"

"I think we'll have to ask Gregson," Addison answered with a smile.

I wanted to be the one to talk to Gregson and there would be no arguing with me. The only problem was, when I went to knock on his door, a strange woman answered.

"Is...Greg...here?" I stammered, struggling to look past her. Gregson was quite old; perhaps he'd hired a housekeeper.

The woman shook her head no, but continued to stare at me. She was a handful of years older than my mother, with deep crow's feet around her dark brown eyes. Her hair fell in a long silver braid down her back and she squinted at me, her forehead wrinkling with recognition. "I've seen you someplace," she murmured.

"I'm not from around here," I said, stepping backwards down the stairs.

"No, not here," she agreed. "But somewhere. You famous or anything?"

Most people recognized my headshot from papers and local magazines that ran insider stories on *Food Porn*. I wasn't about to tell her that I ran the underground provocative magazine. She struck me as the conservative type. I'd probably give her a heart attack. "Nope," I assured her, sliding my hands deep into my coat pockets and hurrying away.

Once back at the house, I spoke to Frank, who informed me that Gregson had moved into a retirement home up in Green Bay not long after his wife, Grace, had passed. He didn't have a phone number. While it was easily tracked down by Mika and James, I decided that speaking to Gregson in person was the smarter way to go. Addison insisted on going with me but I waved her off. She was the only one, other than myself, of my motley crew that my family knew. One of us needed to stay put and keep everyone calm. James quickly offered to go in her stead and I found myself agreeing to his company. I wasn't sure if I was grateful that he'd offered, specifically, or if I was simply in need of a warm body by my side as I uncovered answers I wasn't totally sure I wanted.

John and my parents awoke a short time later. They entered the kitchen, Rachel trying desperately to disappear behind them and avoiding all eye contact. Together, we all went into the garage for the latest on the search efforts. By now, of course, I was nearly positive that Riley wasn't missing amongst the snow drifts. I still wasn't sure where she was, but I was pretty sure she hadn't been killed and tossed by the wayside, nor had she been kidnapped and then left outside to freeze. Still, I couldn't say anything and risk blowing what little cover my friends and I had. The search efforts needed to continue as we drew closer to solving Rachel's riddle.

As the nine of us stepped into the heated garage, I noticed a person I didn't recognize setting up a row of pizza boxes which had just been delivered, free of charge, by the local mom and pop shop. That was the great thing about small towns. People always pitched in the tiniest things, often making all the difference to those at the eye of the storm.

"How sweet," my mother exclaimed, hurrying over to heap plate after plate with hot food, as only a mother can do.

"Thank goodness," my father muttered, alluding to my mother's poor cooking skills. He winked at me, even as my brother lightly punched him on the shoulder and scowled. My brother hated when my parents ripped on one another. When we were younger and so many of our friends had parents going through divorce, my brother was convinced that our parents were one nag away from calling it quits. He'd never quite grown out of his fear, either, despite the fact that Ma and Pop had recently celebrated 31 blissful years at a cabin in Okoboji. I hadn't pressed them for details, but that didn't stop my dad from trying to inform me of their trysts in the woods, the movie theater, the restaurant bathroom, etcetera.

As Frank filled us in on the search efforts, he slowly handed over clipboards, notes and a stack of maps to my father, who would be taking over for a few hours while Frank went home to catch some much-needed sleep. "You folks find anything that we can use?" he asked James and Mika.

"No, sir," Mika responded easily. After Rachel had

scurried off, our group had decided to keep everyone outside of the original conversation in the dark about the curious exchange with Rachel, as well as all of our growing suspicions about Gregson's involvement. We didn't want to generate false hope in my parents or my brother, and we also didn't want additional law hands in the already crowded pot. Plus, Rachel seemed uncomfortable with telling us much of anything, which made us uncomfortable enough to keep our findings quiet. As strange and frustrating as she was acting, her distrust of anyone outside our circle had seemed legitimate. On top of that, if she'd wanted my family to know everything that Addison, Janet, Mika, James and I had been made privy to, she'd have told them already.

Rachel shifted uncomfortably behind Mika. "You alright?" John asked her, concern filling his voice. His forehead wrinkled as he gently took her by the arm, as though she might faint.

"Fine," she promised him with a tight smile, gently patting his hand. Janet eyed the pair, exchanged a look with Addison, and then me. One of us might need to jump in and steer the conversation towards less dangerous waters.

"You're sure?" Frank asked Rachel suspiciously, twitching his mustache. He looked curiously to Mika, studying him. Mika stood poker-faced. Frank turned to Addison, and then Janet, before leveling his gaze on me. I stood as still as possible, worried that the slightest twitch would alert him that we knew more than we were letting on. Poor Frank. I hated keeping him and my father in the dark. They were the two that I ran to as a little girl. As an adult and a woman, it was my turn to protect them.

"Positive," Rachel promised him brightly, turning her smile on full-wattage. Frank again looked from me to Rachel and then back to me. I offered him a small smile, but stopped short of a wave. He'd definitely think something was up if I waved.

Frank gave Rachel one last glance before turning back to my father. Gripping my dad's hand and giving him a quick, one-armed hug, he whispered, "Good luck. Call me immediately if you hear anything. I mean it."

"Will do," my father responded into Frank's shoulder. As Frank walked out of the garage, he zipped up his jacket and adjusted his wide-brimmed hat. We watched him disappear down the block and around the corner before anyone spoke again. My father looked down at the mess of documents he had just been handed and studied them closely. "Well, it looks like our house and John's house have both been searched thoroughly, as has the two-mile radius surrounding both residences. Next steps will be to expand our search radius when the teams shift in about-" He checked his watch and rechecked Frank's schedule that was handwritten on a clipboard. "Thirty minutes."

"What can we do until then?" John asked.

"You can eat," my mother responded, handing both him and Rachel a plate piled high with piping hot pizza.

"Ma, we're not-" he started, trying to shove the plate away.

"Eat," my father demanded of him. "I need you and Rachel both to take care of yourselves when and where you can."

I switched my worried gaze to my brother. He looked much older than his 30-something years in that moment. I can't imagine being a parent who loses a child. I could barely comprehend losing a niece.

Over the next half hour, people began coming back and checking in from their search assignments. No one seemed to have news, good or bad. They'd apologize, find their families and hug one another tightly, having been reunited in light of such terrible circumstances. Some would grab pizza. Others simply walked to their cars, promising to return after getting some much-needed sleep.

New assignments were handed out as new individuals trickled in. These people were both well-rested and warmly bundled, prepared to take on the bitter cold temperatures, hoping to find Riley and bring her home. I found myself feeling terrible for not speaking up and stopping the search operation. After our conversation with Rachel in the kitchen, my gut was screaming in frustration. Riley wasn't out there, we were wasting our time and the time of every townsperson showing up to offer help. Still, the cover remained necessary.

While my parents and brother were distracted getting

everyone saddled up with search assignments, Rachel stepped to my side. "What can I do?" she whispered.

"You can tell me the truth," I told her with a sigh. I turned to look at her and took in how fragile she appeared. There were obvious crow's feet that I'd never noticed before. Her eyes were so tired that the bags beneath them could have passed for bruises. Still, I willed myself to not feel sorry for her. It was looking more and more like she was the reason behind this whole mess and I was done being jerked around. I didn't like being taken advantage of and it seemed like Rachel had somehow morphed into the queen of manipulation.

"I can't," she said shaking her head.

"You don't trust me?" I hissed.

"I do!" she said quickly. "Of course I do, Marian. It's just that- I shouldn't run my mouth. Again."

I stared at her hard, but she didn't continue.

"It might be best for you to wait at your house," Janet said, cutting the tension with her kind voice as she stepped towards us. "I can walk you there if you'd like, Rachel. That way, if Riley returns home, someone will be there waiting for her."

Rachel never broke eye contact with me. She continued to stare, unblinking, as she nodded to Janet's suggestion. All three of us knew that Riley wouldn't be returning home so easily.

When the two went to relay their plan to my parents and my brother, I grabbed Addison's arm and dragged her into the house. James and Mika were hot on our heels. Closing the door behind us, I turned to Addison. "She's convinced that she caused Riley's disappearance."

"How do we know she didn't?" Mika asked.

I felt my shoulders droop. "We don't," I admitted. "But we do have a lead thanks to Addison. Gregson."

"A breadcrumb trail," Addison agreed with relish. "These are my favorite. They always lead you somewhere you don't expect."

"Because you've solved breadcrumb trails so well in the past," James teased her, referring to when Addison had concluded that he and Mika were my killers.

"I don't think that Rachel actually knows where Riley is," I told them. "But I think she knows who took her daughter. Or at least, why her daughter was kidnapped. And Gregson will, too."

"Why won't she just tell us?" Addison asked.

"That, I'm afraid," I responded grimly, "is what we have to find out. And I don't think we're going to like it."

James and I didn't call ahead to schedule a visit with Mr. Gregson. I relied on hope that he'd instead recognize my name and simply agree to see us. Sure enough, when we offered our names at the nurse's station, Mr. Gregson eagerly agreed to a meeting, despite the fact that he didn't recognize both names. "Marian Moyer!" he exclaimed when I walked in the door. His apartment at the assisted living facility was small but functional. It contained a small kitchenette, a living room crammed full of Mr. Gregson's treasures he'd collected over the years, a large wheelchair accessible bathroom and an equally large bedroom. He tottered over to me and gave me a tight, boney hug. "This must be your husband?" he asked me of James, turning and holding out his hand for a shake.

I blushed. "No, no. He's just a friend. This is James."

"Oh," Mr. Gregson responded, sizing James up and down. "Well, that's too bad." James smirked at me as he shook Gregson's hand. We followed our host into the living room. "How can I help you today?" Mr. Gregson asked. "I hope you don't mind my saying, but I was terribly surprised to hear that you'd stopped by for a visit. Green Bay isn't exactly a quick drive from Milwaukee."

"I was visiting my parents," I told him quickly.

"Everything is well, I hope," Gregson said carefully as he leaned over to flip on a table lamp.

"Not really," I responded. "My niece is missing."

"Young Riley?" Gregson asked. His face looked surprised, but his voice didn't echo the sentiment. I could tell that James had picked up on it, as well. "That's terrible. I'm sorry to hear that."

"We actually need your help," I told him. "We have a few questions to ask you, if you're up for it."

"I can't imagine how I can be of help, but ask away," he answered, bewildered.

"Do you know Rachel Moyer?" James asked politely.

Mr. Gregson looked taken aback, but recovered quickly.

"Well, of course," he told us. "That's Riley's mom." We watched and waited, willing him to continue. "Lovely girl," Gregson added, awkwardly. "She's sweet. Helped get my things organized after my Grace died so that I could move up here. Nothing left for me in that town." Gregson allowed himself to become very small and I almost felt sorry for him. Almost. He'd said a few things that triggered additional questions in my brain.

"What kinds of things?" I asked gently. "I don't recall you and Grace having a lot of stuff."

"Books and clothes mostly," Gregson responded. I felt myself perk up a bit. Rachel had mentioned books. Gregson seemed to notice the change in my demeanor. "Nothing special. Just lots of old used things I needed to get rid of. Less stuff to take." He patted his armchair.

"You gave the books away?" James asked. "All of them?"

Gregson paused and appeared to be thinking hard. As he spoke, it was slow and deliberate, as though he was very aware of his words. "I had her sell all of it. For cash. These places are expensive to live in, you know. My social security check barely covers the rent."

James nodded and pulled a small notebook and a pen from his shirt pocket. "Any ideas where she sold them to?"

"I didn't ask for receipts," Gregson scoffed. "Rachel's a good girl. She wouldn't hide money from me."

"That's not what we're suggesting," I assured him.

Gregson crossed his arms and studied me carefully. "Then what exactly are you suggesting, my dear?" His twinkling eyes turned cold and dull. I felt a chill rise in the pit of my stomach. This old guy was luring me dangerously close to the deep end and I had a feeling I couldn't swim in his waters.

"Just wondering if you happened to know the name of the place she sold to," James said easily as I stammered for words. "That's all."

Gregson seemed to accept this and his kindness returned, softening his features. "Some place in Chicago. She was headed to the city for a bachelorette party for a friend of hers. Said she'd sell it all while she was down there."

"But you can't remember the name of the place?" I asked skeptically, finding my voice.

"No," Gregson assured me. "I can't." His voice was once again cold steel. After a few seconds, he steepled his fingertips and leaned forward in his chair. "Has Rachel done something wrong?" he asked suspiciously.

"That's what we're trying to find out," I told him. "Would you mind if we gave Rachel a quick call to see if she can recall the name of the bookstore?"

"I don't think you need me on a phone call," Gregson chuckled nervously. "Why don't you just ask her yourself when you get home? So if that's the end of your line of questions-" Gregson hefted himself out of his chair with a grunt and began to stagger towards James and I, trying to shoo us out his front door.

I didn't budge, but narrowed my eyes. Something was definitely not sitting well with me. I pulled out my cell and dialed Rachel's number, which I knew by heart. "I just think she'd love to hear from you," I assured Gregson, putting the call on speaker phone. "Now that she's no longer in your employ, it can simply be a call for pleasure, rather than business."

"Two things you should never mix," Gregson said hurriedly. "Listen, it has been lovely catching up but it's getting late and I really think you should-"

"Hello?" Rachel said, answering my call. "Em? Is everything okay?"

"It's great!" I chirped. "Listen, James and I are just sitting here with Greg Gregson and he told us that you were sweet enough to help him pack up and sell a few things on his behalf, so his move to the assisted living facility was easier."

"Retirement home," Gregson snapped.

"Anyway, he was just trying to recall the name of that store you sold all of his used books to. He thought it was some store in Chicago." I waited and stole a glance at James, who was grinning wildly at my boldness.

"Rachel," Gregson growled quietly.

"Rachel," I said smoothly. "Tell me. Now. We've come too far to hit another dead end."

There was another moment's pause. "The Quill," she finally answered quietly.

Something flashed in Gregson's eyes, but it was quickly gone. His face immediately crumpled. "Ah," he said quietly. "That's it."

I looked from Gregson to James and shrugged. "Well, I guess that's all. Thanks for your help, Rachel. Have a good night."

"You, too," Rachel said before the line went dead. I wanted to reach through the phone and hug her. The confession hadn't been easy, I was sure, but it was another crumb. Gregson had obviously sworn her to silence. While before I'd have laughed at this, I was beginning to think Gregson was a dangerous man, despite his age. I didn't blame Rachel for being cautious.

Mr. Gregson tottered back to his chair and sat silently for a few moments, his head resting against his hand. "Old brain," he said, tapping his head without glancing at us.

"I understand," I said, my voice more cool than I thought it was capable of.

A lingering silence rose between us. Finally, Gregson shakily pushed himself back to his feet and he walked quickly to the front door. Opening it, he turned back to James and I. "I think you'd better go now," he muttered quietly.

I looked at James, who shrugged. It was likely that we'd uncovered all that we could from Gregson, for now. Even if he did know more, we'd have to investigate a little further before we had more questions to ask him. I walked slowly for the door and gave Gregson a cold, hard stare as I passed by. "Great to meet you," James muttered.

"I'm sure I'll be seeing you again," Gregson admitted.

"I feel as if that's likely," James said with a nod.

We'd been back on the road for about 45 minutes when my cell phone began to ring. It took me several seconds of patting various pockets within my purse to find it. When I finally located it, I quickly answered with a breathless "hello?"

"Break in the case," Addison said hurriedly.

"Oh, God. Did you find her?" I asked, running my free hand worriedly through my hair. James turned to look at me, a question filling his eyes.

"No," Addison responded quickly, and I shook my head at James. "But a follow-up to the ransom arrived at your brother's house."

"In the mail?" I asked confused.

"Hand delivered," she responded. "To your brother's house."

I shook my head in disbelief. "What? Who would do that?"

"That's just it," Addison said. "Rachel won't tell us."

"What do you mean she won't tell you?" I cried. "Can't someone reason with her? John?"

"She didn't tell them," Addison revealed. "She only told me. Called. She made me swear I would only share with you. I assume she had to know we would tell the other three."

"What is going on?" James hissed, trying hard to keep his eyes on the road but glare at me threateningly at the same time. I filled him in quickly. "What?" he cried in disbelief.

"I know!" Addison screamed on the other end of the line. Pulling the phone away from my ear, I switched it over to speaker. "It's typed again."

"What does it say?" I asked her.

"To have the money at the diner where Rachel works at 7:30pm and for Rachel to be the one to deliver it," Addison said.

"And Riley?" I asked.

"Doesn't say," Mika admitted, coming in on the conversation. Addison must have us on speaker, as well.

"Let me get this straight," James said loudly, keeping his eyes trained on the road. "We're supposed to come up with the full ransom within the next few hours, leave it with

Rachel and have her hand it over, without a clue as to Riley's whereabouts?"

"That about covers it," Mika told him.

The silence stretched for what seemed like far too long before Janet broke in. "Do you think we should tell Frank or your dad about this?" Her voice sounded tinny and very, very far away.

I immediately shook my head, even though they couldn't see me. "We have to protect Rachel," I responded. "Addie, she asked that you keep this to yourself for a reason."

"She's the one with three million dollars," James argued. "If anyone needs protecting, it's probably your niece."

Addison sighed. "Marian is right," she grumbled. "If Rachel really is in on this whole thing, she's probably our best bet of finding Riley." Pausing for a moment, she continued, "It sounds like you're in a car. Are you on your way back from Gregson's?"

"We are," I assured her.

"Did you find anything?" she asked, suddenly bold with curiosity.

"Quite a bit," I teased. James and I alternated sharing the strange scene that had unfolded back at the retirement home with Gregson.

"Weird," Addison breathed when we'd finished.

"Quite," I answered.

"The Quill," Janet said from far away. "We have to go, I guess. In person. I'll go. I'll drive myself down to Chicago tomorrow."

"Why not tonight?" James asked.

"It's too late," Janet assured him. "It's nearly a four-hour drive to Chicago from here. They'll be closed by the time I get there, I'm sure. I'll leave early tomorrow, though. Before dawn."

"What about the ransom?" I asked. "What do we do about that?"

"It feels funny," Mika told me. "Something about how quickly it appeared. How cagey Rachel was with the details and not telling us who delivered it. How she was home alone when it happened."

"You're sure my parents and John don't know about it?" I asked them.

"Positive," Addison and Janet responded together.

"Maybe it's some kind of setup?" James asked. The silence stretched long and loud. "Good grief," James finally said, rubbing his temples as he steered our car along. "What the hell happened to cases that were easy?"

"They've never been easy," Mika reminded him. "They just weren't quite this messed up."

"Criminals are getting creative," Addison chimed in. "It's the only way they'll make headlines."

"Then why don't you people stop giving them attention?" James asked.

"You people?" I heard Addison's voice prickle with indignation. "Do you mean reporters?"

"More or less," James replied.

"I provide a service," Addison roared.

"Hey!" I said, cutting off a nasty string of cuss words that exited Addison's lips next. "Can we please try to focus? There's a ransom due in a few short hours. Between that and the bookstore tomorrow, we might be able to wrap all of this up and bring Riley home alive in the next several hours. We have to work together, though. As a team. United and all that nonsense." I paused and yawned, suddenly very sleepy. I wasn't sure how long I'd been awake today, but it felt like far too long. "We'll be back in about another 40 minutes or so," I assured Addison. "Cool down. Do some deep breathing."

"I suppose we're going to work on coming up with over 60 grand in secret," she responded sarcastically. "It's going to be darn near impossible."

"Which is just the kind of possible I like," said Mika, just before I clicked off. At least someone over there was positive about the unfolding situation.

James and I rode in silence for a few moments. As I peered out the window at snow-filled, empty fields, I felt my whole being begin to crush under the weight of hopelessness. Hopelessness is a terrible emotion. If I could banish one feeling from the human variety, it would be that one. I always thought that fear or sadness were worse, but I was wrong. Hopelessness eats at your soul in a way that no other emotion can, allowing those other pesky feelings to leak into the empty holes and nest there, willing you to feel more and more depleted, until the ugly stepsister, Giving Up, makes her grand entrance. Hopelessness sucks.

James seemed to sense this and reached an arm across the cup holders, setting a hand on my leg. "We'll find her," he told me sternly. "And she'll be okay. I promise."

I felt myself smile a little. "You're not supposed to promise a victim's family anything. Crime 101."

James shrugged. "I don't really like the rule book. I'm more of a renegade."

I grinned. "So I'm learning. Still, we need to be reasonable about the possibilities here." The whole situation was exceedingly twisted. I didn't want to admit it but there was a strong possibility that I wouldn't be a huge fan of the outcome. Just because someone hadn't kidnapped Riley and left her for dead in the bitter winter didn't mean she hadn't been hurt or worse, somewhere far and away from her loving family.

"Well, Darlin'," James said easily, "I've known you off and on over the years. But one thing I've learned is that I've never known you to be reasonable about anything." He paused and frowned. "And I absolutely mean that as a compliment."

I set my hand atop his and turned back to stare out the window, a worried frown on my face, and hoped with all of my heart that he was right.

We returned home to little progress having been made. My parents were out in the garage, collecting information from people who had returned from their searches, creating new assignments and struggling to stay warm near the space heater. Nearly the whole town had been studied by this point, but my parents were desperate to find their granddaughter. Desperation could make you unreasonable. Unreasonable could mean searching the same spots again and again, hoping for missed clues. I'd seen unreasonable many times as I'd photographed crime scenes. An unknowing victim's family would come home to ambulances, body bags and thick yellow tape. They'd attempt to charge into the crime scene, not believing that someone they loved was dead, despite the evidence laid out in front of them.

John was off searching for Riley, while Rachel was still waiting at home in case Riley turned up there, even though both she and I knew that, that wouldn't happen. I looked and looked for Addison, Mika and Janet, but couldn't find them anywhere. Having no clue where they'd run off to, I texted Addison, asking that she and the others meet us at my brother's house. It would be easier to keep things under wraps there, away from volunteers and prying family.

When we arrived, I knocked on the front door. It was the first time I'd ever knocked. Normally, I just let myself in their house. Somehow, that didn't feel right this time around. Rachel opened the door quickly and cast a suspicious glare at us. She turned to check behind her. The others, I suspected, were already there. Then she spun around to face us again, anger contorting her face into an ugly expression. "I can't believe you put me on the spot like that," she hissed. "Calling me with Gregson right there! He's gonna-"

"What?" James asked her calmly. "Kill you?"

Eventually Rachel turned away, not bothering to confirm or deny James's suspicions. "Everyone is in the living room. This way," and she motioned for us to follow her, as though I hadn't been into her living room hundreds of times before. On the couch sat Addison, Janet and Mika. They each held a mug of tea and were munching on frosted cookies. "Riley and I made those. Yesterday, before she was grounded," Rachel said quietly. "We were going to surprise John after dinner. He's been working so late in the mailroom, now that we're in the holiday season."

I sighed, my anger with her dissipating. I no longer cared if she was playing me. I was tired of guessing at her intentions. "Do you have any idea where she might be?"

Rachel shook her head. "I swear. I have no idea where she is. If I did, I'd tell you."

"But you know who may have taken her," Janet said from her place on the couch, between munches. "Was it Gregson?"

Rachel shook her head. "I can't. I can't tell you anything. Please."

"But why?" I pled, taking one of her hands in mine. "We're alone here. No one will know."

"Because I don't know anything more," she said simply.

I dropped her hands in disgust and shook my head. "You know more than you're letting on," I challenged her.

Rachel continued to stare at the floor, silent.

"Okay," I said, taking a deep breath. Clearly that conversation was going nowhere. "Let's focus on the ransom drop that's supposed to happen tonight."

"We're not going to be able to lock down the money in time," Addison told me quickly. I immediately felt deflated. How much more could go wrong?

"There's no way for anyone to get it from the local bank or police department without someone blabbing," Mika said simply.

"This town is too damn small," James added.

"Stupid Agnes Thorton," Addison mumbled. "How much longer is she going to be alive? She was old when we were kids, Mare."

"It is frustrating," James agreed, "but at least three people in this room have that kind of money sitting around." He looked to Mika. "Why can't you or I just do the draw? Agnes Thorton has nothing on us."

"But we both use banks local to the city," Mika reminded him. We'd have to drive all the way back to Milwaukee to withdraw. No ATM will give us that kind of cash. And there's no way to make it to Milwaukee and back by seven."

"Rachel uses a national bank," I told them.

"But she'd need to transfer the funds, which would take time," Mika said. "On top of that, she'd have to withdraw from her local bank. Which again broaches the issue of blabby Agnes telling everyone that your sister-in-law is suddenly rolling in the dough. That's one risk we can't take anyone around here knowing just yet- including your family, Marian."

"So what do we do?" I asked, looking from one face to the next.

"Simple," James said with an easy smile. "We bluff."

I'm not particularly fond of bluffing. This is due, in part, to how horrible I am with doing it. Honesty is the best policy anyway, right?

We spent the remainder of the afternoon hashing out details around the drop. As 7pm inched closer, we went through the final layout, just to make sure that everyone had their assignments correct. Mika and Janet were to go in first and request a table. James would follow a few minutes later and sit alone at the kitchen bar. Rachel was to enter by herself, carrying a paper bag filled with Monopoly money, and sit near James. She would want to be close enough to him that he could hear any conversation that transpired between she and Riley's potential kidnapper, but far enough away that he didn't intimidate anyone to the point of not appearing. He was rather intimidating looking, after all, even with his gun hidden beneath his long but chest-hugging t-shirt.

Addison would be waiting in a car by the entrance, while I sat in my own vehicle at the exit behind the diner. We weren't exactly sure who or what we were looking for, but we knew that if we somehow lost Rachel in this mess, we were screwed. It was better to spread out and keep watch as best we could.

Once everyone was in place, I got a text from Mika.

She's inside.

In other words, it was time to start paying attention. I settled back in my seat, crossed my arms and waited. The back door opened a few times and I jumped up in my seat, squinting through my window, but it was always a staffer coming outside to smoke or drop a bag of garbage into the dumpster. One time it was a cook and one of the waitresses, taking turns pushing one another against the cold brick establishment, their tongues tangled in a slobbery mess as their hands ran over various body parts of the other. The cook was short and round while the waitress was tall and thin with messy bleached hair. I couldn't make myself stop watching. I was so distracted by the mess that I didn't realize how close I'd leaned in over my steering wheel. I accidentally honked, scaring all three of us. The chef wheeled around quickly and both of them took an opportunity to cast a dirty look my way, the waitress even flipping me the bird before she flounced inside after her secret lover.

The spikes of adrenaline, each followed closely by an inherent lack of action, were taking their toll. After about an hour, I could feel myself nodding off. In desperation, I cranked up the only rap station I could find. It was fuzzy and faded, but it was all that I had. I cursed myself for not grabbing a coffee. Observation was for the birds.

Somewhere in the midst of a fourth helping of bitches and hoes, there was a loud knock on my driver's side window. I yelped, then turned to see James, holding a cup of steaming hot diner coffee. My hero. Turning down the radio, I immediately reached to roll down my window. "Having a good time?" he smirked, handing me the styrofoam cup.

"What happened? Did he open the bag?" I asked. Taking a sip of the coffee, my eyes closed in pleasure. The slightly burnt hazelnut flavor rolled over my tongue and deep into my throat. Cheap diner coffee is so close to my mother's own attempt at the drink that, for a moment, I was home. As I swallowed, I was hit with a wave of nostalgia. I felt terrible not informing my parents of our plan that evening. We'd more or less hustled off without saying anything to them, or to John. Still, I'd feel worse if I'd gotten their hopes up tonight only to disappoint them again — which appeared like it would be the case. If Rachel thought this would turn into anything, she'd have informed everyone of the second ransom note. My parents weren't old but they certainly weren't sprightly. I wasn't sure how much more bad news they were capable of handling and they had been handed quite a load over the last day or so.

"He was a no-show," James said. "We've been waiting for over an hour. Mika called it."

I allowed the news to sink in. "So where does that leave us?" I asked. Just then, my phone began to ring. Pulling it out of my coat pocket, I saw that my mom was calling. "Hold that thought," I said. "Hi, Ma."

"Where are you kids? I've been worried sick," she

moaned. "I come in from the garage and you're not there. I look in your bedroom and you're not there. I call Rachel's house and no one picks up. Everyone left us."

"We're working on the case."

"You're what? Does your father know? No one tells me anything," she cried. "Your father is calling off the next round of volunteers. They're saying sub-zero temperatures tonight. He doesn't want anyone getting frostbite. What if Riley gets frostbite? Why has no one been able to find my baby?"

"Truthfully, I don't think Riley is out there," I admitted quietly. I heard my mother gasp — as though this possibility hadn't dawned on her — and raced to calm her nerves. "I'm sure she's somewhere warm, though, that's all I'm saying."

My mom sighed heavily, wanting to believe me with everything she had. I didn't blame her, wishing that I could just believe myself. Just then, the passenger door opened and James slid in. "Cold out there," he mumbled quietly.

"Who is that?" my mother asked.

"It's just James," I assured her.

"You need to tell me more about this young man," she said.

"Not now," I said through gritted teeth.

"Please?" she begged. "Distract an old woman. I need something good to happen to our family. Are you seeing each other? He's a real stallion."

"Ma, that's gross."

"Your father- I've always been grateful. He's a real stallion himself, if you know what I mean," she said with a giggle.

The image in my head was too much. I gagged a little. "I have to go."

"Well, when are you coming back? Surely you kids must have a lead or something by now. You're all young, intelligent people involved in various branches of the law. You wouldn't run off and scare me half to death for nothing. What did you find? What do you know? Tell me. Please."

"We're doing everything that we can. I promise," I assured her. "We'll be back soon. I think." I looked to James for confirmation and he nodded. "James says we will be back soon."

"Are you kids hungry?"

"We don't need-"

"I'll just put together some sandwiches."

I sighed. Food was my mother's response to everything. There would be no point in arguing with her. "Sounds great. See you in a bit." We disconnected.

"Did you understand what she meant when she said your father was a stallion?" James asked me with a conspiratorial wink.

"Shut up," I grumbled. "What do we do now that the drop was a no show?"

"We go home and regroup," James admitted. "Hope something comes of The Quill tomorrow. Otherwise, unless Rachel can give us something new to go off of, we're back to square one."

"Riley has been missing over 24 hours, James," I said quietly. "You know how this works. Especially with missing children. We have to find her soon or we may never get the chance."

James stroked my cheek. "We'll find her," he assured me. "I promised you and I meant it."

In that moment, it was all I could do not to kiss him. We stared at one another for a long time, his hand gently touching my face. I felt my breath quicken and my heart begin to pound. I watched him, waiting, licking my lips in anticipation. Was it too much to ask for a little sympathy kiss? Sometimes a girl just needs some comfort. Eventually, though, James turned away and I felt my stomach sink with disappointment. "They'll wonder where we are," he said quietly.

I sighed quietly and nodded. Slipping the SUV into gear, we nosed towards my parents' house. The drive was short but we managed to fog up the windows with heavy, unanswered breath. At one point I couldn't see out the windshield and I found myself wondering why he hadn't kissed me. When he and I arrived home, everyone else was gathered around the kitchen table, munching on peanut butter and jelly sandwiches, including my brother, who was tightly holding Rachel's hand. "Not half bad," my father promised me of the sandwiches between chews. Hesitantly, I took one from the tray and bit into it. You wouldn't think it would be possible to screw up something as simple as a peanut butter and jelly. Still, my mother is more than capable of doing just that and has proven it on a number of occasions. Don't ask.

"Any leads Mr. Moyer?" Addison prompted my father between chews.

My dad shook his head. "She's not out there," he told us assuredly. "We'd have found her by now. I know she's not out there." There was a pause and a sigh. "I haven't been able to get in touch with Frank to let him know I called off the search for tonight. Left messages."

"He's probably sleeping," I assured my dad. "Running that size of an operation in such cold weather really takes a lot out of you, I'm sure."

My dad nodded. "I just wish that whoever wrote that ransom would follow up."

I shot a look to Janet across the table, who coughed loudly. Addison began to pat her worriedly on the back.

"What?" my mother asked, perking up. Her motherly instinct was buzzing and she knew something was up. I was sure of it. "What is it?"

"Ma-" I started.

"It's nothing," Addison told my mother pleasantly, continuing to pat Janet. "Bread just went down the wrong pipe, I'll bet."

"Addison," I warned.

"Marian," Addison responded with a leveled stare.

"I'm okay," gasped Janet, clutching her chest.

"There was a follow-up ransom," James blurted out.

"What?" my father cried, dropping his sandwich and leaning across the table towards James. If we were in an old Hollywood film, he'd have grasped James by the lapels and shaken him. "There couldn't have been. Why wouldn't anyone tell us? We're police!"

Rachel moaned quietly and dropped her head into her hands as John gave her a sharp look. "Did you know about this?" he asked her angrily. She didn't respond.

Mika glared across the table at James, who just shrugged. Janet sat quietly, taking long sips of water. Addison leaned back in her chair and crossed her arms tightly as she studied my parents, who were white-faced and silent. I put my hand on James's arm as a sign of unity. I had his back. It was time to come clean. Sort of. "It's true," I told them. "That's where we were earlier. There was a drop amount. And a place. And instructions."

Some color started to come back to my father's face. His cheeks pinked with excitement. Riley or no Riley, crime was what the man lived and breathed for. "And?" he asked.

I shook my head. "They were a no show."

"No," my mother said quietly, raising her hand to cover her mouth. "My poor Riley. My baby."

"I can't believe you didn't tell me," John snapped at Rachel. Suddenly, he pushed himself away from the table and stood with a disgusted look. Wiping his face with a napkin, he tossed it back on the table and began stalking towards the hallway. "Thanks for dinner, Ma. I need to go home and get some rest." A few moments later, there was the sound of him putting on his shoes, then the loud slam of the front door.

"I- I'm sorry," Rachel stammered, standing and scurrying into the hall. "I need to go, too." A few seconds later, we heard the front door squeak open and shut, as Rachel screamed John's name into the cold black night. I imagined her running after him. He'd shake her off and continue to push towards the house. She'd try again. It would continue like this until they reached their front door. I'd seen it happen that way a million times.

Heavy silence descended upon the table. No one ate. No one drank. No one spoke. My regret began to feel heavy when I noticed how small and fragile both of my parents had become in those last few moments, the excitement leaving my dad nearly as quickly as it had come to him. Finally, Addison broke the silence. "We weren't going to say anything," she growled to James. "We were going to keep them out of it so that- that- THIS! Didn't happen!" She gestured wildly to my parents, who were sitting dejectedly, clutching each other's hands.

"Addison Mae Dawes," my father said quietly. He was one of few people who could use her full name to make her listen. Almost instantly, her back went rigid and she cast her eyes downwards. My father continued. "I so appreciate your desire to protect Lou and I. But if you kids ever, ever keep us in the dark again, I will kick you into next Sunday. Do you understand?" Addison nodded. "What else do you know, then?" my dad asked the table.

"Since the drop didn't pan out, our last lead is a used bookstore down in Chicago. Janet is headed there tomorrow."

"How did you find your lead?" my dad asked us, confused. "And why haven't you been involving the local police? This is why we have so much trouble trusting you people." He glared menacingly at James and Mika, who had the decency to look contrite.

"The problem is," Mika began in a soft voice, "we don't know who to trust within the local PD. There's a reason Rachel was coming to us and not the police."

"I'm really confused," my dad said, holding up a hand, swiping grape jelly from his beard with the other. "Rachel was giving you kids information that she didn't give us? Why?"

"We're not sure," James told him. "But there are a lot of possibilities."

"What kind of possibilities?" asked my mother, rubbing her temples. "This doesn't make any sense. And none of it sounds like Rachel."

"We'll explain everything," Mika promised her quietly. "But you have to promise us that all of this stays in this room. There can be no further involvement of the local police." He looked at my dad. "I understand how difficult that will be for you, Sir, but at this time, it's how it has to be."

"We promise," my parents answered unanimously as they

leaned forward. "Now," my father prompted. "Tell us everything."

I finished filling my parents in on all of the details we'd withheld. I started with the secret bank accounts, then went on to expose Rachel's unintentional lead, Gregson's misstep, our call to Rachel, the additional ransom note and the failed drop. At the end of it, my father leaned back in his chair and crossed his arms. Closing his eyes, he appeared to be deep in thought. We all stared, waiting for him to speak. "What if Rachel wrote the ransom notes herself?" he finally asked. "No suspicious fingerprints were found. John seemed just as shocked as Lou and I were. He clearly knows nothing."

"If that's true, if Rachel wrote both ransom notes, then why?" asked Addison, looking up from the table. She looked much calmer and far less red in the face than she'd been just a few minutes before.

James shrugged. "Maybe she's responsible for Riley's disappearance."

My mother shook her head. "I don't believe it," she cried loudly, turning to me. "And shame on you, Marian Louise, if you believe a word of that malarkey," she added, wagging her finger towards me.

"Lou," my dad said gently, covering her hand with his, gently lowering it to my mother's side. "I hate to say it, but given the evidence, Rachel should definitely be considered suspect." My mother frowned at him, causing deep lines to crease her cheeks and forehead, but she didn't argue. We all sat quietly, waiting for this revelation to settle in. After a long stretch of silence, my father spoke. "I think," he said, "I think that we all need to get some rest."

"But Riley-" my mother started.

My dad took her hand again and squeezed it gently with a knowing look. "I trust our daughter. I trust her friends, even if I don't appreciate how they've kept us in the dark. If Marian thinks that we need to solve this case without bringing police resources further in, we need to trust her. And we need sleep to be on top of our game. You and I should try to get more rest. Reset our internal clocks. Get back to our regular routine."

Mika nodded. "I agree. Let's all get some sleep and come at this again in the morning, once it's had a chance to marinate."

"I haven't even been awake that long," my mother protested. "I'll never be able to sleep. I have to do something."

"You could help us get set up," I suggested. "We all need beds for the night."

A while later, my mother had put fresh sheets on John's bed, made up the couch, and lumped together several pillow nests on the floor. Much to my parents' dismay, James and Mika gave up both beds and the couch so that all three visiting women had a comfortable spot to lay our heads. My dad eyed both men suspiciously as they lingered in the hallway, unsure of who had the privilege of my floor versus who was going to be in Addison's room.

"Whatever," I finally muttered in frustration, pushing past both of them to stalk into my childhood bedroom.

"You don't even care?" my father called after me. "Are you dating both of them, or something?" I closed the door loudly behind me as I went to change into my pajamas.

"Well?" My father called through the door. "Are you?" When I still didn't answer he muttered "Christ," and I imagined he was giving himself the sign of the cross as well.

"Don, leave her alone," I heard my mother murmur. I could picture her putting a calming hand on his chest, the way she often does when he starts to get worked up.

After I'd changed, I pulled back the layers of blankets and sank comfortably into my old bed. It sagged slightly in the middle and I found myself melting into it, not caring that the lack of decent springs hurt my lower back. A small pile of teddy bears was stacked neatly near the drab white wall. I grabbed for my favorite. He was missing large patches of hair and had, had to be sewn up in several spots. When Addison and I were younger, she'd wanted to be a beautician. One day she'd actually taken the shears to my teddy bear collection. My mom had been able to salvage most of them, but their battle scars would forever linger. I sighed deeply into the teddy's fur. "I'm so overwhelmed," I told him quietly. "I feel like the entire day has just been a colossal waste of our time."

Just then there was a gentle knock on my door. "May I come in?"

"Yes," I answered, sitting up, clutching the bear tightly to my chest. I was wearing a t-shirt but there was still something intimate about a man coming into my room when I was so barely dressed. James stepped inside and closed the door quietly behind himself. I smiled shyly but didn't lower the stuffed animal.

"Disappointed?" he asked me with a devilishly handsome grin.

"No," I admitted. And I wasn't. The revelation surprised me, considering how hard I was crushing on Mika.

James carried his bag to the corner of the room and softly dropped it to the floor. Then he began to unbutton his shirt, facing the wall. I watched him, mesmerized. After he peeled his shirt off, he folded it neatly and laid it across his bag. His shoulders rippled slightly under the soft moonlight. I gulped and clutched my bear tighter. Next, James unhooked his belt buckle before unbuttoning and unzipping his dark-wash jeans. It was suddenly very warm in my room and I fought the urge to fan myself. Folding his pants, he stacked them neatly on top of his shirt, then walked over to the bed. He stood over me for a few moments, but didn't do much else. "What are you doing?" I finally asked.

"Getting in, Kitten. That alright with you?"

Nodding, I scootched myself closer to the wall as James slid himself between the sheets. We both lay on our backs, staring at the ceiling for a moment. I continued to hug my teddy bear to my chest, both of my hands tucked neatly beneath my armpits. No way was I making a move. Addison's words from the previous night echoed loudly in my head.

After a few moments of mutual silence, James rolled to face me and propped himself up on his elbow. He watched me carefully, saying nothing. I continued to study the ceiling, even as his gaze on me intensified. "What?" I finally asked, snapping my head towards him. I was feeling incredibly self-conscious, but trying not to make it too obvious.

"Nothing," he sighed, laying back down. He rolled to face the other direction and I shifted my gaze upwards again. An old poster of Justin Timberlake was still sticky-tacked on the popcorn ceiling, smiling down at me with those adorable, bleached curls. Why couldn't I go back to being a kid in the '90s, when everything was simple and my worst fear was getting a pimple? Come to think of it, that was still a pretty regular fear. Granted, it was nothing compared to laying next to a gorgeous specimen who couldn't man up enough to make a move. Did I even want him to make a move? I wasn't sure. I really liked Mika. I wasn't totally ready to make my final call.

"Screw it," James muttered suddenly. With that, he turned, took my face in his hands and kissed me. Hard.

Teddy was squashed between our bodies, straining to keep them a few inches apart. He was clearly unhappy that he'd been replaced.

Eventually, I pulled away. "What are you doing?" I gasped, breathless.

"What any red-blooded man in his right mind would do," James responded.

"I can't sleep with you. Not here. Not in my parents' house!" I hissed frantically.

"I'm not going to take advantage of you," James assured me. "But I fought to be in here with you tonight and I'll be damned if I don't prove it. If I don't at least kiss you, I may as well sleep on the floor." With that, he kissed me again and I felt myself slowly melting into his chest, my hands sliding around his back, clutching it tightly. My defenses were down. He was a damn good kisser. And all of those rippling muscles weren't too bad either.

At some point during the night, James and I had fallen asleep wrapped in one another's arms. I awoke to my phone alarm going off, alerting me that it was 4am and time to go wake Janet. I was sure she was capable of waking up all on her own, but call me a control freak. It was my niece's life we were talking about.

As quietly as I could, I peeled back the covers and went to crawl over James. I was straddling him incredibly carefully when he reached up and gripped my hips, pulling me down against his groin. It was rock hard and very, very stallion-like. God help me. "Morning," he murmured with a wicked grin.

"I have to turn off my alarm," I whispered nervously.

Expertly, he ground up against me, pulling hard at my hips. "Right now?"

Moaning quietly, I tried to wriggle from his grasp. "Yes," I answered, trying to push myself off of him. He was strong. Hadn't I just been admiring his muscles last night? Now I was cursing them. Them and all of their rippled glory.

"You sure?" he asked. Slowly, he rose from the bed and wrapped his big, burly arms around my upper back. Leaning towards me, he slowly licked the length of my neck, pausing just beneath my chin. I felt my breath quicken as James growled quietly.

My resolve was dissipating when the bedroom door creaked open. "Marian, I was wondering if you wante- oh, God! I'm sorry! I'm so sorry!" Janet whispered embarrassed, pulling the door closed tightly behind her.

James instantly let go of my hips and I rolled out of the bed, falling hard onto the floor. Flailing for a moment, I finally managed to grab my phone and silence it. With a dirty look to James, I stood and chased Janet out into the hallway. I finally caught up with her just outside the bathroom, where she'd begun unpacking her shower supplies. "It's not what you think!" I told her as quietly as I could, tugging at the hem of my t-shirt and hoping Addison and Mika weren't awake to hear us. I was suddenly very aware of how little clothing I had on.

"Hey, I'd totally go for the other one, but it's not my call," Janet teased.

"Oh my God," I moaned, dropping my head into my hands. "What am I thinking trying to date both of them at once?"

Janet's eyes nearly fell out of their sockets. "You're dating both of them?" she hissed. "Are you joking?" I shook my head miserably. "Girl! You're crazy."

"I know," I told her. "I've been doing this for a month and I'm no closer to a decision." I paused. "Well, that's not really true. But every time I think I want to spend more time with Mr. Dark and Dreamy, James actually steps up and does something unexpected."

"Did you sleep with him last night?" she squealed.

I shushed her and pressed my ear against Addison's door. Nothing behind it seemed to be stirring. "No," I finally admitted. "I haven't slept with either of them."

She let out a low whistle. "That's disturbingly impressive."

"I hate to admit this, but I'm proud of myself," I giggled, thinking about how gorgeous both of the men actually were.

"You're coming with me today," she said with a pat on my arm. "We have a lot to talk about and I could use a buddy on such a long drive."

Nodding, I shooed her into the shower and closed the bathroom door. Leaning against it, I again tugged down the hem of my t-shirt and bit my lower lip as I imagined going back into my room to get dressed. No question — I might never come back out.

Freshly showered, we jumped into Janet's rental and started towards Chicago. James had, thankfully, fallen back asleep so grabbing my stuff for the day hadn't been an issue. Janet and I were well outside of town before we came across a pit stop that served breakfast. That was the big challenge with small-town life. Starbucks was, surprisingly, not on every corner. We stopped for coffee and bagels before aiming ourselves back towards the great big city of Chicago. The sunrise was a beautiful wash of purples and oranges and pinks, dancing off of fluffy clouds. I found myself wondering what we would find — if anything — at The Quill, and prayed that we weren't too late.

Without warning, my phone began to ring. Assuming it was someone back home, wondering where we'd run off to so early, I quickly answered, not bothering to take in the caller ID. "Hello?" There was some crackling and a garbled voice on the other end of the line. My heart began to pound. I sat up quickly and pressed the phone harder against my ear. "Hello?" I asked again. More crackling. More garble. "Riley?" I asked. "Riley, is that you?"

"Ipson," I was finally able to make out.

"Ipson?" I asked. I looked to Janet, confused. She'd been struggling to listen in, so I switched my cell over to speaker just as the static and garble broke free and my signal grew clear as day.

"It's Carly Ipson! Hello? Can you hear me?"

"Yes, I can hear you!" I shouted, clutching the phone tightly.

"Hey, Carly! It's Janet," my driver called cheerfully. "How's it hanging?"

Carly laughed on the other end of the line. It was melodic and infectious. "Isn't that what they say in California? Thought you'd moved to Florida, friend."

"Great to hear from you," Janet said, "seeing as how you weren't much help to Marian in her last unsolved mystery."

"I was on vacation!" Carly cried.

"I know, I know," Janet teased. "Three weeks in Europe and completely unreachable."

"Though in hindsight, Barry always gave me the creeps," Carly admitted.

"Good to know now," I told her dryly.

"So tell me what's happening," Carly said. "Marian, you just asked for me to call. Is this about Barry again?

Because if you need testimony, I'm glad to say whatever I need to, to ensure that, that nutcase goes away for a really long time."

"It's not Barry," I sighed. "I wish it were."

Carly let out a low whistle. "Then this must be really bad."

I didn't really know Carly from just some random Joe on the street, but I felt myself trusting her instantly. She had a calming personality. Plus Janet liked her, which was good enough for me. Janet and I took turns filling her in over the next few minutes. "That's all that we know," I told Carly, finishing.

"What can I do?" she asked us. "I'd love to help, but I really have no idea how. Unless-"

"Unless what?" I asked her eagerly. I was ready for some new ideas, considering the only ones my group had come up with were hanging from a thread.

"Well, you said that that old guy- Gregson- was affiliated with some used bookstore down in Chicago. Ever think that maybe Riley's kidnappers took her there? Chicago, I mean. It might explain why no one has been able to find her in your hometown, Marian. I bet I could get some Chicago buddies to look into it."

"Why didn't we think of that?" Janet asked, me, excited. "Carly, what do you need from us?"

"Can you email me photos of anyone that you think could be involved in this mess? Your niece. That Gregson guy. Rachel. Anyone that may have been down in that area."

"I'll have someone back home do it," I assured her. "That's a great idea. What's your email address?"

As she rattled it off, I wrote it down as best I could, given the bumpy road. We were trekking through some well-packed snow, which wasn't making our drive very smooth.

"I can't make any promises," she said before hanging up. "But at least it's something."

Janet and I both thanked her profusely. She promised to meet me for coffee when things were settled and I was back in town, and then we signed off. For the first time since I'd found out Riley was missing, I felt hope seize my heart.

"What's on your mind?" Janet asked me. We'd been moving along in comfortable silence since Carly's phone call. Now we were on the outskirts of Milwaukee, just a short hour and a half from our final destination.

"Just how messed up this whole thing is," I admitted, sipping at the last of my coffee, which had gone stone cold. Somehow, coffee always tasted more bitter when it was cold and I felt my tastebuds cringe. Janet nodded sympathetically, so I continued. "You always say it'll never happen to you. I do it all the time when I'm photographing grisly crime scenes. But here we are." I paused for a moment and turned to stare out the window as I asked my next question. "What if this whole thing really is Rachel's fault? What if all of this was building up and no one noticed or bothered to care? I'd have never pinned anything like this on my sister-in-law, but now? Now I honestly have no idea. This could destroy my family, you know?"

Janet reached across the car and squeezed my arm. "You can't think like that. We're just speculating but, the truth is, everything we've thrown out is just a theory."

I nodded. "I know. You're right. I'll just be happy when this whole this is over and Riley is home safe."

"Me, too," Janet said quietly. She moved her hand back to the steering wheel and we drove the rest of the way to the big city in companionable silence.

Just outside the Chicago city limits, my phone began to ring again. This time, I checked to caller ID. It was James. "Where the hell are you?" he asked when I answered. "I fell back asleep and when I woke up, you were gone."

"I'm with Janet," I told him. "I was already awake and she needed company. It's such a long drive. Plus, it's my mess, you know?"

"Oh," he answered simply. There was a pause and I could tell he was debating asking me another question. I looked at Janet and smiled. "Spit it out, Cowboy," I told him.

"Did I upset you?" he asked worriedly. "Did you leave because of how things went after your alarm went off?"

He sounded so concerned that I almost laughed. Almost. "No," I finally told him. "I promise."

"Then I'll see you when you get back in a few hours?"

"Count on it. And by the way, I have an assignment for

you and Mika."

"Anything," James assured me.

I took a moment to explain my call with Carly and shared her email address with him. "The most up-to-date photos you can find," I said. "I'm sure my mom even has some of Gregson."

"Why would she?" James asked. I could almost hear his brow wrinkling in confusion and I fought a smile as I imagined it.

"It's a small town thing," I assured him with a shrug he couldn't see. "I'm sure he's in a family photo at a town picnic somewhere."

"Call us if you come across any new information at the bookstore," he said.

"We will," Janet shouted, having heard every word of our conversation. With that, I clicked off. "He means well," she murmured, turning to look at me briefly.

"I know," I admitted, tucking my phone back into my pocket. "But Mika does, too."

"Must be rough," Janet teased as I shrugged helplessly. "Well," she said, eyeing me critically, "if we're going on looks, I'd have to say that Mika has that whole dark and smoldering thing going on, which, as you know, is kind of my thing." Janet's husband, Rob, was nearly six and a half feet of gorgeous Brazilian with the sexy accent to boot. "But that whole sensitivity thing really gets me every time," she admitted.

This didn't surprise me at all. Sensitivity was Janet's

middle name. Were I ever in a sticky situation that Addison wasn't present for, with her fierce looks and spitting wit, I'd want Janet, with her level-headed demeanor and kick ass attitude. I'd seen her chase down and tackle a suspect or two, some of them three times the size that she was. It never seemed to matter. The girl was kick ass.

Janet's husband, on the other hand, was much more of a worrier and had an incredibly difficult time making quick decisions. I adored the man, whom I'd been lucky enough to meet and spend some time with on more than one occasion, but Janet, without a doubt, wore the pants in their relationship. In fact, when her husband was offered the amazing opportunity in Florida, he had agonized over the decision for days. This being in the middle of a frozen Milwaukee winter. Janet was the one who finally called into his boss and said they'd take the assignment. Rob just couldn't seem to do it.

"Don't you get tired of running the ship?" I asked curiously.

She shrugged. "Sure, but that's about the time that he takes over. I like being in charge. Seventy-five percent of the time, that is," she laughed. "And when I need a break, Rob steps up. It's not like he's incapable, it's just not his primary way of handling things." As we eased off the interstate exit and paused at a light, she turned to stare at me critically. "The thing is, you may need something totally different than what I need. You're not me."

"I don't know what I need," I told her softly.

"Sure you do." She smiled and tapped my chest. "Listen to that little voice in there. You'll find the answer to everything. Except, perhaps, the meaning of life."

I closed my eyes and tried hard to listen. "What if I don't get a response?" I mumbled.

"It comes," she promised. "Sooner or later, you'll just know."

We'd gotten turned around on the Chicago streets several times. Additionally, neither one of us was used to as much traffic as the big city had. It was a shock to both our systems, especially after having spent the last several hours in such a small town. Eventually, we found The Quill, tucked off a quiet corner, and even scored a nearby parallel parking spot, which is pretty much unheard of in a city as large as Chicago. When we went to open our car doors, my stomach growled loudly. Janet laughed and checked her watch. "We're here about 20 minutes early," she told me. "May as well walk to that pastry shop we passed and grab a bite."

"Sounds good," I agreed, slightly embarrassed. A few minutes later, we'd worked our way through the line and were retrieving our items from the counter. Janet checked her watch again. "It's showtime," she told me, walking fast towards the front door. I followed in hot pursuit, trying to balance my coffee in one hand and a pastry with various fillings and toppings in the other. We made our way down the crowded sidewalks, eating as we raced along. About half of my pastry dropped to the sidewalk as we hustled along, and a murder of crows took full advantage. Hearing them caw gave me the willies and I struggled to walk even faster, slipping and sliding as we went.

I'd just popped the last of my second breakfast into my mouth when Janet cut a sharp left and we dipped into an alley. "Where are we going?" I asked her, nearly sliding past across the snow covered ice.

"Shortcut," she promised. Once through the alley, we curved right and paused, smack dab in front of the bookshop. Stopping, we glanced over the elaborate gold lettering that spelled out the store name in the front window. The inside looked dark and crowded, but a small sign on the door read "OPEN" in bright, green lettering. Taking a swig of my coffee, I went to tug on the handle. "Wait," Janet said, grabbing my arm. When I looked at her confused, she shrugged. "I just have a weird feeling," she told me. Glancing left and then right, she motioned for me to follow her. Back in the alley, she moved along the long side of the building, her hand softly touching the brick.

"What are we doing?" I asked her.

"Looking for another exit," she told me. "Just in case. Do you see anything?"

I gazed down the length of the wall and shook my head. "There's nothing here."

"There must be an emergency exit somewhere," Janet mused. Rounding the corner to the back side of the building, I heard her shout, "a-ha!" Jogging after her, I glanced around the corner to see some large scaffolding framing a rusty, metal door. She tested the doorknob as hard as she dared. "Locked," she acknowledged. With a glance at the scaffolding, she frowned. "Doesn't look like they're redoing anything. Wonder why this is here."

I let my trained photographic eye wander. Just above where the scaffolding ended was a brand new security camera. Janet was still checking out the area around us, so I tapped her shoulder and pointed.

"Weird," she said. Inspecting the roofline, she pointed slightly further down the building. "Another one."

"They are really expensive looking," I said, observing their make. "Why would a used bookstore in the middle of a decent neighborhood in a busy part of town need such high-tech security cameras? Who would even try something here?"

Janet shook her head, then seemed to think of something. "Were there any cameras around the front?" she asked.

When I shrugged, she reached around to her back and lifted her coat and sweater, pulling out a small black handgun. "Woah!" I cried, my eyes bulging. "I had no idea you were carrying that around."

"I decided to bring it along last minute," she admitted. Checking the chamber, she seemed satisfied with the number of bullets. Clicking it back together, she stuffed it back into her waistband. With a glare at the security cameras, she began walking back towards the front. "Let's get this over with."

As we walked the length of the building and back around the front, we didn't notice anything else out of the ordinary. There were also no additional security cameras to be found. With a deep breath, I tugged on the front door, setting off a friendly welcome bell. "I'll be with you in a minute," came a thick, nasally voice from the back of the room. I eyed Janet, who looked just as confused as I felt. Whoever was here certainly didn't sound dangerous.

While we waited, the two of us split up and began wandering the aisles. Books of every shape and size lined tall, wooden cases. What didn't lie neatly in rows on the shelves were stacked haphazardly on the floor. Several white and black card tables were positioned in smaller spaces between the large shelves, and they were also piled high. The ceilings were a dark brown, molded plaster, from which several fanciful chandeliers hung. I found myself pondering just how one could get a ladder positioned to change the lightbulbs with so many books on the floor, when I heard heavy footsteps an aisle over. "Yes?" I heard the same nasally voice call out. "Is someone here?"

"Yes," I heard Janet confirm off to my left. Quickly, I began walking back towards the front of the store.

When I rounded the front shelves, I stopped short. A short, rather portly man that resembled an overweight George Clooney was stationed in front of a desk, breathing hard. I noticed that behind the piles and piles of books stacked on the desk was a large, antique cash register, as well as a stack of plastic bags and what looked to be an old, leather bound billing ledger. "Can I help you?" he asked me, pulling out a hanky to wipe perspiration from his forehead. One thing was certain. He didn't sound like George Clooney. I found myself cringing whenever he spoke, so confused my brain was by the massive difference between his appearance and his voice.

Just then, Janet rounded the corner and stopped short with a look of surprise. She recovered quickly however and I went over to shake the man's hand. "Mr.-"

"Cork," the man responded. "Ernie Cork. You can call me Ernie."

"Ernie," I began, closing the gap between Janet and I. He turned back to me after shaking Janet's hand, startled, as if he'd already forgotten that I was there. "I'm Marian. This is my friend Janet. We were hoping to ask you a few questions."

A look of fear crossed Ernie's face but he dropped it quickly and busied himself with refolding his hanky. "How can I help you ladies? Do you have a book for evaluation? I usually don't start that service until the lunch hour."

I shook my head and glanced around. No one else seemed to be present except for us. I couldn't imagine why he'd turn down business. "This just looks like a typical used bookstore," I told him.

Ernie stood rigid, but said nothing. He looked from me to Janet and back to me. "It IS just a typical used bookstore," he stuttered.

"Some fancy looking security equipment you have out back for that, Mr. Cork," Janet said, putting on her tough cop face. Sliding one hand into a pocket, she took a step towards him. "Why is that?"

"Can never be too careful," he told us, evenly. "This is a big city. Never know who is going to show up. Try to take advantage of a small business operation like this."

"Just seems odd that you don't have any cameras out front or inside," Janet mused thoughtfully as she glanced up, scanning the ceiling. "If people were stealing things, you'd think they'd run out the front door, not through your stock room."

"Cameras are very costly," Ernie said defensively, crossing his arms across his large barrel chest. "I can only afford a few at a time. Maybe I just wasn't thinking with the placement is all. And what were you doing behind the store any way? I thought you needed a book evaluated."

"I never said that," Janet answered. "You did." I could see pinpricks of sweat popping up on Ernie's thick, pasty arms. It was starting to soak through his blue polo, which was just a smidge too tight around his middle and barely missed his waistline. A blob of pale, hairy belly protruded over Ernie's tightly buttoned black slacks and also appeared to be slick with sweat. "You seem nervous," Janet noted.

"I'm just not sure what this is all about," Ernie shot back. "But I have some inventory I need to get to, so if you have something you'd like to ask..." He didn't seem very confident in his challenge but still allowed it to hang heavily in the air.

This was getting us nowhere quickly. I decided to step in and play good cop. "We heard that you buy used books."

"Obviously," he snorted, gesturing around.

I resisted the urge to throttle him. Here I was trying to help him from getting steamrolled by Janet and he wasn't even appreciative. Gritting my teeth, I continued. "Let me rephrase. We heard that you purchased some books from a guy named Greg Gregson. He would have had a girl come in on his behalf. Rachel Moyer."

Ernie dropped his defensive stance and eyed me suspiciously. "I thought you were coming later," he said after a few seconds. He turned to give Janet a dirty look. "Didn't have to scare me like that," he told her. "And no one told me that there would be two of you."

Confused as I was, my stomach was instantly filled with butterflies. I glanced quickly to Janet and could tell she was feeling the same. We were onto something. "Sorry about that," I told him slowly. "I just thought my friend here could, erm, help."

"You weren't supposed to be here until ten," Ernie muttered, lumbering towards the back of the store. Janet quickly closed the gap between us and gently pinched my arm, excited. I bounced a bit in place but said nothing. Together, we started to follow him down the aisle. "Hey!" he cried, turning to us. "You know the rules. No one touches the merchandise. And no one gets to see where I keep it. He said you're newer so I'll cut you some slack." He gave Janet the stink eye, which she returned wholeheartedly. "And no friends next time, either. You're lucky I don't rat you out. That's how nice I am."

Janet glowered at him menacingly. "I'm sure," she whispered. "You seem the real proper, straight-laced, type."

Slowly, Ernie turned away from us and continued towards the back of the store, alone. When he was out of earshot, I whispered, "What do you think it is?"

Janet shrugged, bewildered. "But somehow it all connects back to Rachel and Gregson. That much we can prove."

There was loud banging in the back of the room, followed by a thump and a string of cuss words. A few minutes later, Ernie emerged, carrying a stack of leather-bound books. They each had to have been three to four inches thick and the pages looked to be gold-embossed. I wasn't sure why he wasn't struggling more with the load, until he reached out and dropped the pile into my arms. Janet went to catch me but there was no need. The books didn't weigh over two pounds altogether. Surprised, I looked to Janet and back to Ernie. "What-?" I started, but Ernie cut me off.

"Here, here," he said, ushering me over to his desk and clearing off a space. He motioned for me to put the books down and, when I did, he grabbed one off of the top. "I know you need to check out the merchandise before you can take it back to the warehouse. Honestly, it wouldn't hurt me to double check. Gave them the wrong stuff last time. Was lucky they let me live, you know?" He laughed like the punishment he'd been expecting sounded normal. It could only mean one thing. We were dealing with some serious thugs.

My stomach dropped. I looked to Janet, who seemed just as shocked as I was. Even before Ernie opened the book, I knew that it was going to be hollow. I also knew that whatever was inside the hollow was going to be something I didn't like. Sure enough, Ernie pulled out a thick plastic bag filled with a curious white powder. "Satisfied?" he asked, without opening the baggie. He shook it in my face. "Want a sniff?" Opening a drawer he pulled out a razor blade, a grimy dollar bill and a streak-free mirror. "I won't tell." Janet and I shook our heads and Ernie shrugged, dropping his kit back into its place. "Couple of goodie two-shoes," he muttered. Securing the substance back inside the book, he stacked the pile back into my arms one by one.

"You guys really scared me," he said candidly as he began ushering us towards the door. "For a second there, I thought you were cops with that whole 'I have to ask you a few questions' routine. Really great stuff. And you," he said, wagging his finger at Janet. "You really look like a cop with the hair tidy and off the shoulders like that, and the professional outfit that looks like you tried." He turned to look at me and wrinkled his nose. "You didn't really fool me, though."

I started towards him, but Janet grabbed my shirt collar and tugged me back, forcing laughter as she pulled me towards the front door. Suddenly, we heard the bell placed above the door ring merrily, signaling that another customer had entered. "That's funny," Ernie grumbled, pushing past Janet and I roughly. "I wasn't expecting anyone today other than you." I nearly dropped the stack of books I was carrying as Ernie's large body shoved me into a wall. I shot him a dirty look, which he never caught. He was too busy trying to figure out who had arrived. Hopefully it wasn't whoever he'd been expecting when we'd walked in.

"Could be an actual customer," Janet told Ernie dryly as he lumbered away.

Ernie seemed to find this hilarious and he turned back to Janet, grinning. "You're funny, too. I don't get many customers. Why do you think I got into business with Gregson?" He patted one of the bookshelves fondly as he walked past it. "Almost lost this place once. Couldn't afford the mortgage." He turned again to look at us. "Bet you both probably know what that's like, don't you? No one gets into this business because it's glamorous. We all owe someone, don't we? We all need to get by."

Ernie was being incredibly conversational all of a sudden. Like he was chatting with old friends. I was just about to try to pump him for some final information, when we rounded a shelf and came face to face with a tall, bald, muscular man dressed head to toe in black. He so closely resembled Mr. Clean that I had half a mind to giggle, but managed to stifle it. It was just as well, because as soon as he caught sight of Janet and I, his face twisted into an angry scowl. "Who the hell are you and where do you think you're going with my books?" he demanded.

The tall, bald man clenched his hands into fists and stood directly in our pathway to the door. I shot a worried glance at Janet, who was remaining cool as a cucumber. Trying to take a cue from her book, I sucked in a deep breath and stood stock still, trying hard not to give away the fact that I was terrified. I didn't even blink.

Suddenly, a large furry dog that looked like a cross between a Saint Bernard and a German Shepherd began lunging at the glass door, slobbering all over it. The animal was leashed to a mailbox outside and clearly belonged to the large, angry man in front of us. I was sure it was trying to defend its owner, the bald man, and basically wanted to rip our faces off. Plus, that whole adage about dogs kind of looking like their owners? That seemed to be the case. It was easy to tell that they belonged together.

Ernie quickly cut in, slapping his forehead. "I've got your books in back, Shannon. I totally forgot you'd asked to come pick up this morning." Shannon didn't seem amused and I found myself stifling another giggle. The large man with biceps as big as a gorilla's head did not strike me as a "Shannon." Ernie stuttered on, unsure of himself. "These are the new helpers- er- I've already forgotten your names, I think. Sorry. Was it Ma-"

"Gloria," I said quickly, cutting him off. No way did I want either of them knowing our real names if they were drug thugs. "And this is my friend- um-"

"Ja-" Janet began, but I elbowed her in the ribs. "Hannah," she finished awkwardly.

"Jahannah?" Ernie asked, confused.

"And I thought my name was stupid," Shannon grunted.

Janet and I chuckled nervously. "My mom loves romance novels," Janet went on. "Jahannah was a character she loved. The book was called, um, *Gone with the Wind*."

Shannon squinted and seemed to consider this, tilting his head like a dog who had heard a distant bark. Ernie looked puzzled and seemed to sweat harder. "Of Time," I finished, quickly. "Gone with the Wind of Time. Great book. Fast read. Excellent character development."

There was a long, awkward silence, then Ernie nodded, the confused look remaining on his face. "I just must not have heard you right when you introduced yourselves earlier. Glad I didn't try to guess!"

Janet and I laughed a little too hard. When we realized the other two weren't laughing along with us, Janet cleared her throat and I shifted the books that I was holding in my arms, so as not to drop them. They weren't heavy, just large and difficult to manage. "So your name is Shannon?" Janet finally asked the large man with the bald, shiny head. She crossed her arms and waited expectantly for an answer.

"Got a problem with that?" he asked her, taking a step forward. I squealed in surprise and fell backwards into Janet, who caught me and propped me back onto my feet.

"No!" we both said quickly. "Great name," I added, gushing, shifting the books in my arms once again. I could feel nervous sweat popping out on my brow. "I've never met a boy Shannon. Not that you're a boy. I mean, you are a boy but I meant you're more of a man. Not a man boy, though. Like a manly man. Hot man. Not that I think you're attractive. Not that I don't think that you are. You're very attractive. But I have a man. I actually have two men. But not like you're probably thinking. One at a time-"

"We'll get out of your hair," Janet said with a tight smile, cutting me off and taking my elbow.

"But that wasn't an insult because you don't have hair," I quickly added, allowing myself to be led towards the large, angry ball of fur outside. Shannon seemed mildly amused, the corners of his mouth twitching with a smile, even if it never came to full-wattage. Janet and I paused in front of the door and gulped. Each time the dog leapt towards us, I counted teeth. He had to have at least a hundred in there. And multiple rows, like a shark.

After what seemed like an eternity, Shannon stepped next to us, made eye contact with the dog and raised his hand in a signal. Almost immediately, the dog stopped barking, let out a low whine and went to curl up by the mailbox. "Better?" Baldie asked us sarcastically, walking back towards Ernie.

"Thanks," I muttered, looking down at the stack of books in my arms. I wanted to clock him, but it probably wasn't an overly wise move, considering his size. And his large, angry beast that he called a dog.

"Well, I'm sure I'll be seeing more of you two," Ernie told us with a wave. "Great to meet you both."

"You, too!" we sang, as we pushed our way out the front door. The dog growled lowly as we jetted past it but didn't make a move to attack either of us. Scuttling by as quickly as we could, with low murmurs of "nice doggie, good doggie," we hurried across the street to the rental car. Janet opened the back door so that I could drop the large stack of books onto the seat. My arms empty, I hurried around to the passenger side and crawled in. It was all we could do to not squeal away from the curb, drawing further attention to ourselves. Shannon had watched us all the way to our car, his arms crossed, his squint angry. Janet and I remained completely silent, holding our breaths until we turned the corner and were out of sight. Then, in the same moment, we both exploded.

"Holy crap!" I crowed, turning to look at the stack of books in the backseat. "What just happened? What are we supposed to do now?"

"We have to call home," Janet told me, her eyes bright with excitement. "We need to tell everyone what just happened. Gregson is involved in a drug ring."

"So is Rachel!" I told her, slapping the dashboard. "This

is big! Do you know how big this is? It's huge! Monumental!"

"It is big. Really big," Janet admitted. "Ernie said something about a warehouse, didn't he?"

"Do you think that, that Shannon guy might be headed there?" I asked her. "Do you think that that's where they're keeping Riley? It's a long shot but, at this point, I think anything is possible." We were quiet for a moment as we mulled all of this over. Janet continued to drive, but I could tell she'd slowed down significantly.

"Well, call home," Janet finally responded, breaking my reverie. "Seven heads are definitely better than two."

I tried calling my parents' house phone first. When no one picked up, I called Addison's cell. She answered halfway through the second ring. "Well?"

"Are you with everyone?" I asked.

"Yes, and you're on speaker," she assured me.

"Is Rachel there?"

"No," she answered. "Just your parents, Mika, James and I."

I took a deep breath and turned to Janet. I wasn't sure if I was ready for my parents to hear the bad news about their daughter-in-law. "This is looking a lot more complicated that we originally thought," I said slowly, searching for the right words. There weren't any. Besides, with as much as I'd already put my dad through, he deserved honesty. My mom could deal. "Looks like it's some kind of drug ring."

"Not some kind of," Janet said loudly. "It is a drug ring. We've got a few pounds of coke sitting in the backseat as we speak."

I heard my mother gasp and I just knew that my dad was making the sign of the cross. "What are you going to do if you get pulled over with all of that?" my mother squeaked.

"Drive slowly, drive slowly!" my father shouted. "Don't draw attention to yourselves."

"Pop, we're driving fine. Just relax," I soothed.

"How did you walk into that?" Mika asked incredulously. "The drugs, I mean."

"Right place, right time, I guess," I told him.

"Didn't hurt that Ernie was a total moron," Janet chimed in. "I can't believe someone like that would be working for an operation this big. He didn't check us at all."

"Who's Ernie?" James asked.

"He's just a low-level mover from what I can tell," Janet shared. "Got into the business to save his shop. Has some pretty fancy equipment that was just installed. I think he usually dishes drugs through the rear entrance. Not sure why he didn't call us out for coming in through the front save for the fact he thought we were new." She paused. "I hate to say this, but I also think that Rachel could be more involved in this than she's letting on."

"You think Rachel is involved in drugs?" my mother asked, aghast. "That's impossible."

"Sure looks like a possibility," I admitted. "At the very least, it appears that she's involved in moving the drugs from place to place."

"Trafficking," James supplied. "Drug trafficking is the official term."

"There's an official term!" My mother cried out. "Drug trafficking." Her thick Boston accent rolled over the unfamiliar words as she enunciated different syllables until she found some that didn't sound overly harsh. I could just imagine her sitting with friends over a game of Bridge, telling them that Rachel was in prison for drug trafficking almost as though she were asking the ladies if any of them needed another glass of punch.

I allowed the news to sink into them for a few moments before I added, "I think we might have a lead on Riley's whereabouts."

There was a collective gasp. "Where?" my mother nearly screamed. I pulled the phone away from my ear in pain. One thing that my mother had never learned was that you didn't have to shout when a phone was on speaker.

"A warehouse," Janet told them.

"Well, where is it?" my father asked when she didn't continue.

Janet and I looked at each other. "Um. We don't know exactly," I told him. "But it's possible that we can find it. There's someone we ran into down here that we can follow. I'm pretty sure he would lead us right to it."

"No way," Mika cut in. "That's way too dangerous. Where'd you meet him? The bookshop operation?"

"It could be our only shot to find Riley," Janet protested.

"Hold on," my father interrupted gruffly. "You all know that I want nothing more than to find Riley and have this whole nightmare over and done with. But in this case, I think Meeko is right."

"Mika," everyone corrected him.

"Sorry," he muttered. "Anyway, he's right. You girls can't just follow some random yahoo and hope that this person leads you somewhere when we don't have eyes on you. You could fall into trouble and we'd have no idea how to get to you."

"Well, if that doesn't work for you, then we need to come up with another plan, and quick," I responded. Janet nodded and pulled our car into an empty lot next to an abandoned construction site just a few blocks up from The Quill. I unbuckled my seatbelt and leaned closer to her with the phone.

Suddenly, we heard the snap of fingers. "Richard!" Addison cried.

"You mean Kris Kringle?" I asked. Richard was Addison's friend with the Chicago PD who worked in narcotics. I'd met him when Addison invited him up from Chicago to help on the Barry case. He looked a lot like Christmas card images of Santa Claus, including the red rosy cheeks and the bright twinkle in his eyes. Until he faced hardened criminals, that is.

"I'll give him a call. See if he can keep tabs on the two of you until we get there," Addison went on, ignoring my comment.

"We don't need a babysitter," Janet insisted. "And we don't have that much time. Our lead is going to leave The Quill soon, if he hasn't already. It's not like we can just sit around and wait for someone to get here to tail us."

"Just call him and then have him call us for a location," I told Addison. "We can explain where we are. He can track us. It'll all be fine."

"Sounds risky," James mused. "What if we can't get in touch with him right away?"

"Risky is just the way we like it," Janet promised him. "And likely our best shot at seeing if these creeps really do have Riley. We don't have any other leads at this point. We have to try."

"If Rachel was pushing drugs for money, I'll kill her," my dad growled. "If her actions put Riley in danger-"

"Let's not worry about that right now," I said, determined. "We have other things to focus on. And Addison has a phone call to make." After a few short goodbyes, we hung up and I turned to look at Janet. The car idled in the lot, puffing out exhaust and fumes into the freezing morning air. "Where do we go from here?" I asked her. "You're in the driver's seat on this one. Literally and figuratively."

She shrugged and ran a hand over her smooth hair. "I know that it's a dangerous move, but I think that we need to get back to the bookstore. See if Shannon leads us anywhere good if you're up for it. Best case, to Riley. Worst case, it will be another clue, I'm sure. I feel it in my gut. Richard can catch up to us."

I nodded. "You're right. Let's get going." I reached for my seatbelt when, out of the corner of my eye, in the side mirror, I caught an object racing towards us. Swiveling to look behind us, I spotted a large, navy Buick barreling through the empty lot, straight for our car. "Hold on!" I screamed to Janet. A loud crash. Though I was struggling to clasp my seatbelt, my hands were shaking too hard and I missed the buckle. There was impact. A scream. I couldn't be sure if it had been Janet, myself or both of us. I felt the side of my head hit the windshield and then my entire world went black.

I awoke slowly. I was lying on a cold floor in an incredibly dimly lit room. As my eyes adjusted, I tried to sit up, but immediately groaned and collapsed back into a pile of bones. My head was pounding. Additionally, I wasn't totally sure why or even where I was exactly. My memories felt jumbled and fuzzy, but I tried to piece them together anyway.

Gently, I raised my hand and touched the side of my head, which was cold and wet. When I moved my hand to view what was on it, I nearly fainted. My fingers and palm were completely covered in bright red, gooey blood.

"Marian," I heard someone whisper behind me. "Marian, are you awake? Are you okay?"

"I'm awake," I moaned. "I need to lay here for a minute before I decide if I'm okay." I paused and swallowed hard, trying to dispel the metallic taste in my mouth. Running my tongue along my teeth, I sighed with relief. None of them were missing. My tongue sure did hurt though. I'd probably bitten it at some point. Immediately I tensed up. Had I had a seizure? Was I in some kind of hospital? "What happened?" I asked Janet, my head still lying on the ground. I couldn't see where she was. "Hey, come here, will you? Check my head, I can't tell if I'm still bleeding."

"I can't. I'm tied up," Janet responded simply. Just then, I heard the squeaky sound of ropes rubbing against one another. How had I missed that sound before? It was incredibly distinct. Like a violin on its last breath.

As gingerly as possible, I rolled from my back to my side. Slowly, slowly, I twisted my neck until I could spot Janet out of the corner of my vision. She sat at the far edge of our dingy light, covered in shadows. We were clearly not in a hospital. Not even a shoddy one. At one point, it looked like Janice had been gagged, but she'd managed to maneuver the black handkerchief they'd used down where it was wrapped tightly around her lower jaw. Her hands were neatly duct taped together and her entire upper body was coiled with thick white rope, the kind one might find looped between fence posts near a large body of water. Her hair was wild, as if someone had been handling her by it. Her button-down shirt had been ripped away and a dark, seatbelt shaped bruise appeared on her upper shoulder and disappeared under her white tank top. "So you are," I said, with as much of a smile as I could muster. Then, with a cringe, I whimpered, "Ow."

"You've been through worse," Janet said encouragingly. "Remember a few weeks ago when your car blew up? You hit your head pretty good that time, right? On concrete?"

"Yeah, I did," I muttered. "What is the deal with me and cars? I'm going to start riding the bus."

Janet snorted. "Didn't you tell me that back in college you witnessed a knife fight on Milwaukee Public Transit and that you'd never use it again?"

"I'm changing my mind," I grumbled, feeling my aching head again. I hoped that when I pulled my hand away, there would be less blood. There wasn't. I sighed heavily and tried not to gag. Photographing crime scenes was one thing. Experiencing one live was a whole different matter. I didn't have the stomach to witness my own grisly demise.

Janet pursed her lips sympathetically. "I can't even imagine how much pain you're in right now, Em, but I need you to come help get me out of these so that I can bust us out of here." She gestured as much as she could with her hands and wrists.

"Fat lot of imagination you have if you think I can get myself all the way over there," I groused. The simple act of turning my head had made me nauseous. In that moment, 8th grade Science came rushing back to me. My teacher had told us that every part of the human body was connected. Shoulder pain could mean heart trouble. Foot pain could mean your allergies were about to kick in for the season. Bizarre things like that. I'd never actually believed much of that. Now, though? Now, I had no doubt that every single nerve and tendon was somehow fused together purely as a form of torture.

"I just need you to try. Please." Her eyes were pleading. Seeing as how she was tied up and I wasn't, whoever had us locked in here clearly hadn't expected that I would wake up. Or they expected that if I did, I wouldn't be of much help. What they didn't plan on was my level of stubbornness. Few things piss me off more than when someone expects me to fail. Pain or no pain, I'd have to try. Moyer blood runs thick with thoughts of revenge and the triumph of a simple, "I told you so."

Gritting my jaw, perhaps to keep from crying out in pain, or maybe just to keep from vomiting, I slowly eased myself onto my stomach. From there, I awkwardly pulled myself across the cold, hard concrete, pushing with my feet. The first few feet had me slipping and sliding, as my hands were both covered in blood and I couldn't firmly plant them on the floor. I had to stop every foot or so for a deep breath and to wipe away the tears of pain that were blurring my vision. All the while, Janet gently spoke quiet words of encouragement. Somehow, and I'm completely bewildered by how, I eventually ended up at her feet.

"Great!" she whispered. "Now I need you to pull yourself upright so that you can get this tape off of me." She gestured again with her wrists.

It took several attempts, several moans of agony and one dry heave, but I finally made it into a sitting position. Laying my head on Janet's lap and not even caring that I was soaking her pants with my blood and mess, I began to work at the tape. When her hands were free, I used her chair as a pulley and maneuvered myself around to the back. Inspecting the knots, I shook my head, then winced.

"I'll never be able to get these untied," I told her, frustrated. "These knots- it's like someone was a Boy Scout."

"Swiss Army knife. There is a hidden pocket in my back

waistband," she assured me. "I didn't bring you this far to fail now, Moyer."

I slowly felt along under her belt until I came across a hard lump. "Sorry," I muttered, reaching my hand inside her pants and opening the zipper.

"I appreciate that you want to get squirrelly, but this really isn't the time. Plus, I'm married."

"Tease," I threw back, pulling out the knife and finding the sharp blade.

After what seemed like an eternity, I'd made enough cuts in the rope that Janet was able to undo the whole lot of them and free herself from the chair. She twisted and turned until the ropes fell to her feet and she could stand to stretch. Once she was free, I groaned and slowly made my way back down to the floor. Its coolness felt wonderful against my hot, sweaty body. "That's better," I sighed, splaying my arms wide.

"Let me see you," Janet chided, kneeling next to my head and pulling the handkerchief wrapped around her chin down and around her neck. Gently, she parted my hair and inspected what I could only assume was an incredibly ugly-looking gash. It felt huge, even though it was probably rather small. "They cleaned out the glass before they brought you in here," she told me quietly. "Glued you, too, which looks to have stopped most of the bleeding."

"Most of the bleeding?" I scoffed, glancing at my hands, which were caked with blood and dirt from the concrete floor. "How much was there to begin with?"

She took the knife from my hand, folded it and placed it back into her secret zipper pocket. "It probably looks worse than it actually is."

"Can you see my skull?"

Janet smiled and patted my arm. "Thankfully not." We continued to sit this way for a few moments, me splayed out on the floor and Janet huddled over my head, gently touching my arm. "I was afraid you wouldn't wake up," she confessed. "There was just so much blood. I'm no doctor but I thought maybe I'd lost you."

"You're going to have to fill me in on what's happening," I told her. "The last thing I remember, Addison was going to call Richard who was going to then call us. My guess is that, that second call didn't actually take place." I glanced at our surroundings but my gaze paused on Janet's chest. "I don't mean to stare, and you do have a lovely chest, but that's a nasty looking bruise you have on it. My expertise with photographing bodies tells me it's recent."

"Do you remember the car accident?" Janet asked me quietly.

I thought hard, but shook my head. When she didn't say anything, I asked, "Should I be worried that I can't remember we were in an accident?"

"Again, I'm not a doctor, but I assume that, that isn't great," Janet confessed. "But do you remember your name?"

"Clarence," I joked.

"And do you remember that you helped wrestle me out of

some ropes just now?"

"I did?" I asked, feigning shock.

"So I'd like to think that you'll be okay until we can get you to a doctor," she smiled. "It isn't total short-term memory loss."

"And when do you think we can make that happen?" I asked her hopefully. "I'd love a morphine drip and maybe a soft pillow. Oh, and some chocolate pudding. They still serve that in hospitals, right? Maybe a hot dog platter with curly fries?" My stomach began to groan in agreement.

Janet laughed, loud and clear. "I'm not sure." From there, she began to fill in the gaps that were scattered throughout my memory.

Someone had quickly gotten word that two women who weren't supposed to be sniffing around The Quill were. I found myself briefly concerned for Ernie's well-being. If sending someone the wrong drugs had almost gotten him killed, I hated to think what they'd do to him when they found out he'd given away their entire operation.

At some point, it had been ordered to find Janet and I before we were able to spread the word. We were wanted, dead or alive. That's about the time Janet and I were clobbered by a huge Buick. Janet, thankfully, had still been wearing her seatbelt, but I'd unbuckled mine shortly before we were hit. As a result, Janet ended up with some serious bruising only. Meanwhile, I had almost become a hood ornament. Oddly, whoever was driving the Buick had slowed down a bit just before the collision, almost as if they'd wanted us to live. Janet still hadn't figured out who had been driving it. While I could sort of recall the vehicle approaching in the mirrors on our rental car, I didn't seem able to remember so much as a shadow of the person behind the wheel. For all I knew, it could have been the President.

After we'd been hit, two thugs had crawled out of the backseat and pulled us into their car, which was, of course, still running. I once saw a Buick get rammed by a dump truck and the driver walked away without a scratch. Those things are tanks.

One of the thugs had proceeded to drive Janet's rental to this super secret location, probably so that it wasn't left behind for someone to find. Unfortunately, as they drove us away from the abandoned lot, they'd tied a bag over Janet's head. She tried to keep track of the amount of time they drove, as well as all of the twists and turns, but she was convinced that they drove around for a while unnecessarily before we ended up where we currently were. A warehouse.

I had been passed out cold the entire time. A middle-aged, pepper-haired gentleman with wire-rimmed glasses had quickly examined my lifeless body. From there, Janet said, he'd tweezed a bunch of glass shards out of my head and hair, glued together the largest of the gashes and recommended pain relievers, to which everyone around the table had simply laughed. Janet, whose head bag had been removed and was now able to see what was going on, was forced to watch as two creeps searched my lifeless body for weapons. When one of them tried to get fresh, Janet had attempted to hit him but was promptly reined in.

When it was Janet's turn to be frisked, the assholes apparently weren't much kinder to her than they'd been to me. She'd spit on the guy that copped a feelski, which promptly got her struck hard and fast across the face. They'd managed to find her gun, which was hidden in her waistband, but had somehow missed the knife. Probably due to the fact that the pocket was interior and covered by a thick belt on the outside. The man in the glasses, likely a doctor, had asked Janet to remove her shirt so that he could examine her for any pain or bruising. When she'd refused, one of the thugs had promptly wrestled the buttons of her long-sleeved shirt undone, leaving her pissed off and semi-naked. She'd allowed herself to fume silently, not wanting to draw any additional attention to herself.

From there, the thugs carried Janet and I both to the room we were currently in, tied Janet to her chair and left me lying lifeless and alone next to the door. Janet said it had easily been a few hours. She'd screamed for me to wake up until she was nearly hoarse, but I'd never stirred. She'd also scanned the room for security cameras but hadn't seen any. They were either incredibly small and well-hidden, or our room was safe from prying eyes. We were both betting on the former, though it was odd that no one had been in to see us yet now that I was wide awake and Janet was free.

"Any ideas if we're still in Chicago?" I asked her. "Have you seen Riley? Or asked about her?"

Janet shook her head. "No news about Riley. They took my phone and yours, too. Crushed both of them, in case someone could track us with them. We're probably somewhere in the city still. We didn't drive all that long. Maybe near the stockyards?" She paused and sniffed the air. "That's what it smells like, anyway."

"Great. So what do we do now?"

"Well," Janet said, standing and dusting off her pants. "I suppose we could see if they left the door unlocked."

"That's ridiculous," I croaked. "They'd be the worst kidnappers in all of history."

"They would," Janet agreed. "But there's just something about the dumb luck you always seem to have that-" At that moment, Janet reached for the door handle, twisted and yanked the door wide open. Her eyes widened in surprise as she stumbled backwards, completely thrown off balance. "-tells me we should try," she finished, turning to look at me, dumbfounded.

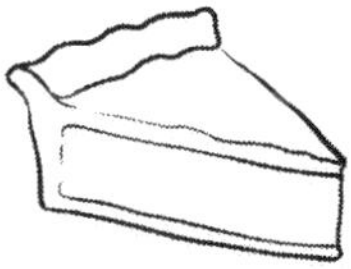

Janet stuck her head into the hallway and looked right, then left. "It's empty," she whispered to me, coming back into the room.

"This can't be for real. It's a trap," I mumbled, still splayed out on the floor. "Someone's sick idea of a trick."

"Marian, we have to check it out," she told me. "What if they're just that stupid, that they would leave our door unlocked? I was tied up. You're clearly not going places."

"Maybe," I said hesitantly. The tiniest movements shot agonizing stings across the whole right side of my head and I squeezed my eyes closed, gasping in pain. "Seriously, though, what if it's a trap? Go all the way out there and they'll probably blow your head off with a bazooka."

"Only one way to find out," Janet said with a grin. "I've been practicing my duck and run, anyway."

I smiled, then shook my head as best I was able. "I can't do it," I told her, my eyes stinging with fat, hot tears which finally spilled over onto my cheeks. "Janet, I don't think I'll be able to walk. My head just hurts so much. Every time I move, I want to gag. What happens if I pass out?"

"I'll help you," she assured me, hurrying over to help me stand. "You can hold on to me. Lean on me." She stepped back over to my side and knelt down, tucking her hands between my shoulder blades and the concrete, as though she was going to push me upright.

Alarm bells began firing off in my brain and I flapped her away. "No, stop it," I cried, not wanting to do any further damage to my already damaged body. "I hate to ask this of you, but I need you to go on your own. I'd just slow you down. We don't even know where we're going out there. If there's even a chance you can get out of here, maybe you can find us some help."

Janet's face was pained but she knew I was right. She leaned forward and gave me an awkward side hug as I laid there, pasted to the ground. "I'm coming back for you," she breathed quietly in my ear. "I promise."

"Don't go Titanic on me, Kate."

"I've been practicing my Oscar speech."

"Shut up and get out of here already."

As she stood with a smile, we heard a loud, slow applause. Janet tensed and turned towards the clapping as I shifted my head to see who had walked in the door. I can't say that I was surprised by our guest, but my stomach still rolled with a mixture of confusion and fury. "Gregson," I acknowledged through gritted teeth. "I wish that I could say it was good to see you, again."

"Ah, Ms. Moyer," he said in a voice that brought sickness to my stomach. I stared him down as best I could from where I was laying. I certainly wasn't in any kind of an intimidating position, but I had been ranked "best angry face" back in high school. Not really a proud moment until just now. Gregson was dressed in a snappy black suit with a red and silver tie hanging loosely around his wrinkled neck. His tiny, bony frame now seemed sharp and menacing. How had he kept this side of himself hidden for so long? When John and I were kids, we used to ride our bikes over to Gregson's house in the summer months, where he and his wife, Grace, would sit on their porch swing and hand out popsicles to all of the neighborhood kids. Had he been this evil back then? Had Grace? "Marian. I'd like to say you look good, but I think we both know that's a lie," he sneered, slowly making his way towards us.

I noticed Janet's hands begin to ball into fists. Frankly, she'd likely be able to take him. Gregson was a good three inches shorter, four sizes smaller, and chances were that he wasn't too quick on his feet anymore. Just as I thought Janet was going to start moving towards him, swinging, two incredibly huge men squeezed through the door, both trying to shove the other out of the way so that they could enter the room first. It would have been comical if it weren't so terrifying. Both men were dressed completely in black and sported biceps the size of my head. One had a thin, brown goatee that looked completely out of place on his chin. Almost as though someone thought it would be funny to pencil it in as some kind of joke while this large man slept. "What is this?" Janet asked, gesturing angrily at the men.

"Oh, now," Mr. Gregson said gently. "What's your name

dear?"

"Screw you," Janet jeered.

"Well, fancy that," Mr. Gregson said in stride. "That's quite a funny name. I'd introduce myself but I'm pretty sure you already know exactly who I am."

"I thought I did," I muttered from the floor, still lying supine, but with my head shifted to the side. "But I guess, how well do you really know someone when it comes to matters of illegal activity? Someone just appears normal and then, poof! They kidnap their neighbors' kid and try to murder her aunt."

Mr Gregson chuckled, practically skipping across the floor to the now empty chair that Janet had once occupied. He sat and leaned close. I shivered with disdain and forced myself over a few inches, despite the excruciating pain it caused my head. "Was that worth it?" Mr. Gregson asked me in a low voice that only I had caught. With that, he laughed long and low and pulled his chair forward so we were practically touching. I'd have bitten him if he hadn't been wearing shoes. That'd teach him.

"Stop it," Janet said, making a move to grab Gregson. As she did, one of the large men standing in the doorway took three quick steps and grabbed her by the back of the shirt. She fell backwards into the man's chest but angrily pushed herself off of him, causing her shirt to rip open even further. A small tear appeared under her left arm. She didn't seem to care. "Don't you touch her," she growled menacingly at Gregson.

"Or what?" he asked teasingly. "You gonna hit me?"

"Maybe not right now," Janet said, turning to stare down the man who still held onto her shirt. She turned back to Gregson. "But eventually, I'll knock you into next week."

"I'm terrified," Gregson responded dryly. Smirking, he stood and walked around my body. I half expected him to kick me in the ribs, but, thankfully, he didn't. Perhaps he still had some empathy left. "How did you think you were going to get her out of here?"

"You're the idiots who left the door unlocked," I muttered. "And who misses a Swiss Army knife?" Janet made a noise in the back of her throat and, had I been able, I'd have slapped myself. They hadn't even known the knife existed. Until now.

Gregson frowned. "Ah, yes- a knife. That's how she managed to get free." He snapped his fingers and the thug holding Janet by her shirt swung her around and shoved her, face first, into the brick wall. Janet cried out in pain as the man frisked her, finally reaching inside of her waistband to pull out the small pocketknife. Tossing it to Gregson, the thug spun Janet back around, leaving her merely inches from Gregson and I.

Angrily, she flailed out her arms and just barely connected with Gregson's jaw, causing him to drop the knife. Janet tried kicking it towards me with her foot but thug number two stepped in and grabbed it just in time. Gregson's head snapped back from the light blow and he grunted in pain, softly rubbing his chin as Janet was subdued by thug one, who had pressed her back into the brick wall, his forearm tight against her neck. "I'll kill all of you if you touch me like that again," she screamed.

"Not if I get to kill you first," the thug holding Janet growled at her, his goatee twitching.

"Manners, Bruce," Gregson told his man, as he walked towards Janet. His eye held an appreciative twinkle for her feistiness. "The two of you make quite a team," he crowed to her. "I'm sure if Ms. Moyer were feeling a bit lighter on her feet she'd have no doubt grabbed the weapon and given you two a bit of an advantage. Not that a small knife will do much damage to my assistants as you can see."

"You're sick," Janet said, disgusted. She wheezed against the large man's arm, struggling for breath, but was unable to free herself no matter how much she hit and clawed at him.

"Truth is, the two of you are far more determined than anyone had thought," Gregson mused. "Especially him. I suppose it could prove useful for you both. In the end."

"Him?" I asked confused.

"Useful for what?" Janet breathed skeptically at the same time I spoke. Her face was beginning to take on a grayish tint.

"No matter," Gregson said with a grin, answering both our questions with no answer at all. He turned towards his goateed thug, who was slowly, firmly strangling Janet with his forearm. I wanted nothing more than to stand up and kick the crap out of all of them, but I could barely lift a finger without wanting to cry. Would they kill her right in front of me?

"Let her go!" I screamed as loudly as I could muster.

"Oh!" Gregson cried in mock surprise. "If you insist." With a snap of Gregson's fingers, the man with the goatee immediately removed his forearm from Janet's neck. Panting, she fell to the floor, clutching her throat, breathing hard.

"Janet," I mewed.

"I'm okay," she insisted.

Angrily, I turned my gaze to meet Gregson's. "Why did you leave the door unlocked and let us try to escape if you knew you were just going to stop us when we tried?" I asked him. "What was the point of all that?"

The thug without the comical goatee shrugged. "We just forgot, I guess. But it was kind of fun for a few seconds there when it looked like the hot one was going to escape," he added. "It gets really boring around here sometimes. It's the same thing every day, you know? Bring in drugs. Count drugs. Send drugs out. Buy some cheap hookers." He shrugged again. "Same thing. Every day. Except the hookers. They usually change." He frowned, his brow furling in thought. Suddenly, he seemed to remember something that surprised him, probably something having to do with cheap hookers, and it made him laugh out loud. When he regained control, he added, "But otherwise, pretty boring."

"At least until you three came along," the goatee guy sneered.

My stomach dropped. I sincerely hoped that he wasn't talking about Riley.

At that moment, we heard a blood-curdling scream echoing off the walls just outside our door. My hair stood on end and I desperately wished that I could rub my arms to fend off the cold fear. Unfortunately, every move that I made just caused my stomach to roll and I was desperately afraid of suddenly getting sick. It would be more than I could handle.

Without warning, I saw two figures push through the shadows. One was just another angry looking, thick-armed thug with a giant nose ring and smudges of black eyeliner. Who knew so many beefy bodyguards existed in the same square mileage? It was almost frightening.

The second person that joined our bedraggled crew looked alarmingly like Rachel.

Sure enough, Rachel came stumbling through the door, holding fast to the back of her head. The man behind her was moving her along by tightly gripping her hair. "Let go of me!" she screamed, trying desperately to pry his hands away.

Gregson sighed and looked at me sadly. "I swear, I don't know who teaches them to be like this. I've always stressed chivalry, especially when I'm having them deal with young ladies."

The three men snickered and the man who had brought Rachel into the room shoved her hard across the floor. Her head snapped forward and the rest of her body tumbled after. Thankfully, she caught her balance just before barreling into me as I continued to lay helpless on the floor. "Was that really necessary?" she asked no one in particular, rubbing hard at the back of her head. At that moment, she recognized the woman being held captive in the corner. "Janet?" she asked incredulously. Slowly, Rachel swiveled towards me and swallowed hard before making eye contact. "Oh, God," she said as soon as I gave her a small smile and a wave. Immediately, she fell to the floor beside me and began inspecting my head. "How much does it hurt?" she asked, carefully setting my head in her lap.

I winced in pain. "Pretty bad," I whispered. "But then, I don't really have much to compare it to. Just that one time my car blew up. And when I was younger, I fell off my bike and face planted." I felt pathetic. You wouldn't think a head wound could wreak so much havoc. In reality, not only did it hurt, but it totally threw off my equilibrium. I felt like someone had dropped a small brick on my head and then fueled me with alcohol. Unfortunately, the buzz had worn off and the awful hangover was in full gear. There's almost nothing I wouldn't do for a painkiller. Including give up Reese's Peanut Butter Cups. For a year. Maybe a month. Okay, a week. A day. I could last one whole day without eating a single Reese's Peanut Butter Cup if someone would just pass along a pain killer.

"She needs medical attention," Rachel begged Gregson.

"She's had it," Gregson informed her. "Only the best. You've met Cooper before. Our doctor on retainer," he explained.

"Let me guess," Rachel said cooly. "He suggested painkillers and you all had a good, hard laugh about it."

"How do you know that?" Janet asked suspiciously.

"Let's just say that when I broke my arm this past summer, it didn't come from tripping down the stairs," Rachel assured her.

"They broke your arm?" I asked weakly. I faintly remembered my mother saying something about Rachel getting a cast last summer, but she'd downplayed it so much, incredibly unlike my mother, that I'd promptly sent a bouquet of flowers and pretty much forgot about it. I was a terrible sister-in-law.

The guy with the goatee shrugged. "It was an accident."

Rachel snorted. "Just like everything else around here."

"How did you keep my mom from freaking?" I asked, ignoring the situation at hand. "She was so calm that day when she called to tell me you'd gotten a cast."

"I may have been present," Rachel answered slyly. "With liquor."

"How did you get here anyway?" Janet asked her. "Last I saw, you were chasing after John."

"I had her picked up on the way home," Gregson smiled. "I was headed this direction. Thought she could use a lift and that John could use a little alone time. Quite a shock I'm sure. For his own wife to betray him so deeply."

"You know that's not true," Rachel said, prickling. "You know that I only did it to protect him. To protect Riley."

"And look how well that's going for you," Gregson sneered. "But perhaps you should keep it up. I'd love to add a few more Moyers to the collection. I'm sure HE wouldn't mind."

"He who?" I asked.

Rachel shook her head. "Ask Gregson. I have no idea. I've never met 'him.'"

"Maybe Gregson is just lying," Janet said, narrowing her eyes. "He seems like the type. Maybe he's just trying to scare us."

"Oh, I don't have to use lies to terrorize you, ladies,"

Gregson said, snapping his fingers. I gulped as the thug with the nose ring lurched forward and seized Rachel roughly by the arm. She squealed and tried hard to pull away, but she was no match for his bulk. He easily dragged her across the floor and pitched her over his shoulder like a sack of flour. My head fell woodenly from her lap to the hard, concrete floor and I cried out in pain. Rachel screamed and kicked, clawing and biting, but the muscular man just chuckled and carried her out the door, slamming it shut behind himself. "Now," Gregson said softly, "where were we?"

"Where are you taking her?" I asked, worried.

"Never you mind," Gregson responded with a smile. "I just wanted you to see her. Briefly. So you'd know you weren't alone and all of that poetic nonsense."

Janet came over to kneel next to me. "What do we need to do in order to get Marian some medicine?"

"Oh, you're willing to do something? Tit for tat, that sort of thing?" Gregson asked with a smarmy smile as he eyed Janet's shirt where it was ripped across her chest. At least her undershirt was still intact. If I'd been her, I'd have clutched what was left of my button down closed and tried to retain a bit of modesty. Janet didn't seem to care in the slightest that some old geezer was totally checking her out. In fact, she just stared back with a bored expression as if she'd been ogled a million times before. Chances were, she had. The girl was in seriously good shape. My mind instantly wandered to the photo shoot just a day or two prior with James and the slice of apple pie. He was in seriously good shape, too. Those arms. Those abs. Those eyes. And to think the other morning we could have done the deed! Had I seriously given up what could have been my last chance ever to get frisky?

I groaned involuntarily and closed my eyes. Janet, mistaking the noise for pain, took on an urgent tone. "Or you could do the chivalrous thing and just give it to us," she challenged Gregson.

"Why?" I cried out angrily, shaking a fist towards the sky. "Why now? Is this so that I hurry up and make a decision?"

"Is she becoming an illusion?" Goatee asked.

"Delusional," Gregson corrected him.

"I'm not delusional, I'm just in need of an orgasm," I vented. "And you," I said pointing at Gregson, "have taken away my chance."

"Both chances," Janet corrected.

"Both chances!" I moaned. "Who would believe it?"

Janet and Gregson stared at each other uncomfortably for what seemed like ages as I carried on, lying on the floor. Finally Gregson turned and nodded at Goatee, who promptly nodded back, turned and left the room. We waited in relative silence, save for my occasional muttered curse, until he came back, holding a small brown medicine container. He handed it to Gregson, who opened it, shook a few times, and eventually held out two white pills to Janet. When she didn't move to take them right away, he gestured eagerly with his hand. "Go on. I won't bite."

Warily, Janet took a step towards him but kept her eyes on his thugs. "What's the catch?"

"No catch," he said. "I just want her to quit talking about orgasms." With a grin, he added, "You asked for pills and I'm giving them to you. As a peace offering. I can be a nice person. When I want something." He glared at me and I squinted right back.

"Okay, you two," Janet said to Gregson and I. "Marian, open up."

I glanced at the pills in her hand, which were roughly the size of my pinkie. "You're kidding."

"It's dry or not at all," Gregson snapped.

I glared menacingly. "Orgasm," I whispered slowly.

With a heavy sigh, he turned and nodded to Goatee again. Goatee rolled his eyes so far back into his head that nearly all I could see were the whites of his eyes. Eventually, he turned to leave the room and returned with a large glass of water. Gregson snatched it away and shoved it towards Janet.

After I'd taken the pills, Gregson stepped around Janet and came to stand directly over me. I refused to look at him. He squatted down and took my chin in his hand, pulling my face every which way until I had no choice but to meet his eyes. I considered closing mine to avoid this horror but decided I probably shouldn't tick him off any further. "I do love your fire," he told me finally. "Trust me, you'll probably need it in here. I can't even begin to imagine the amount of pain you're in." He frowned and seemed to think hard for a moment. "Actually, there was that time Carlos Von Kelsey broke both of my knees with an aluminum bat. Left me in an alley. I almost froze to death before somebody found me a few hours later." I gulped and felt my eyes grow a bit wider with fear. That sounded pretty terrible. I wasn't ready for any more pain.

Gregson grinned and, letting go of my chin, slowly stood back up, his bones popping and creaking as he did so. I couldn't understand how someone who was so old and looked so sweet could be filled with so much evil. "What do you want from us?" I finally asked, unabashed. "I mean, you know what I want. I want my niece, my sister-in-law, my friend Janet here and myself to all get home alive. I want the opportunity to choose between two gorgeous, equally hunky men. I really, really want to eat something packed with carbs and sugar. I want to see Fred."

"Is that another man?" Gregson asked, confused.

"It's my fish," I answered sadly. "Those are all of the things I want. What is it that you want?"

Goatee raised his hand. "I want-" he started, but Gregson cut him off with a sharp look.

Turning back to me, he studied my face for a long moment. "I don't want anything from you," he assured me softly. "Nothing at all."

"That's funny," Janet bit back. "Because for a while there, it really seemed like you just wanted to kill us. If you want nothing, why not just let us go?"

Gregson smiled and clasped his hands behind his back, almost as though he were contemplating a math problem. "You're fiery, too. And pretty." He pointed at her with his thumb and turned to his thugs. "I really like her."

"Oh, shut up," Janet snapped.

The room went quiet as Gregson pondered his next move. I saw Janet eyeing the door, but there was no way past the thugs that blocked her path. They may not need us, but it was obvious we wouldn't be going anywhere.

"Well," Gregson said quietly. "I suppose that I'll leave you both to it. Don't go doing anything stupid, now."

"No promises," Janet responded.

After Gregson and his thugs had left, Janet stood, but then quickly slid back to the floor. "Crap," she sighed. "My leg is asleep."

"Gee, that must really suck," I slurred. The pills had only been in my system for a few minutes but they were having obvious effect.

Janet turned and grinned. "Sorry," she said, patting my hand.

As my head began to feel lighter and lighter, I allowed myself the pleasure of turning it to look around at our dingy surroundings. As it turned out, I hadn't been missing much. "That was weird. With Gregson," I finally blurted out, rolling onto my belly and laying my cheek on the cold concrete.

"Geez, careful Marian," Janet cried, pulling my wild hair out from under the deadweight of my head. "Let's keep the wound breathing, alright?"

"Wound," I said slowly. The word rolled around in my mouth and I giggled. "Wound," I repeated.

"Yes, wound," Janet answered, brushing hair out of my eyes. "Another word for injury." I giggled like a hyena, high on painkillers. "He was in the room when that doctor recommended painkillers. I'm not sure why he suddenly had a change of heart," she continued, ignoring me.

"One can always hope that his conscious suddenly reappeared," I responded, coming to my senses a bit. "He did use to be nice. Would give John and Addison and I popsicles. Oh!" I said, flipping over to my back.

"Cripes! Marian! Stop rolling around like that. You'll hurt yourself again."

"Popsicles sound delicious."

"They do."

"Think they have any here? My lips are dry."

"We can ask next time someone comes in."

I giggled. "Popsicles in prison."

Janet smiled wryly. "I'm glad one of us can see humor in this situation."

I giggled again. "Wound."

We sat in silence for a few minutes. I listened as the sound of our breathing bounced off the cold walls of our prison. There were no windows. The only light was the creepy yellow bulb that hung lonely above our heads, flickering out every so often with a loud buzz.

Eventually, I bored with the quiet and tried to think of something entertaining to do while we waited. I was busy pretending that my hand was an incredibly large shark when, suddenly, Janet seemed to realize something. "The door," she whispered. She stopped and looked around us, as if searching for something.

"What?" I asked her, as one of my hands ate the other.

"Cameras," she whispered. "Do you see any?"

I looked around, but spotted nothing. "No."

"It would make sense though. If these guys were in the same operation as Ernie."

"Maybe they only have cameras outside, too."

Janet seemed to consider this, then shuddered. "It's like that song in that musical back in high school. "Somebody's eyes are watching. Somebody's eyes are seeing you come and go."

"That's terrifying," I muttered. "Both that you remember those lyrics from high school and the song itself." Janet shrugged noncommittally. I resumed my game of hand shark. Flippantly, I said, "Maybe the door is still unlocked. I didn't hear it click after they left."

Janet looked at me confused. "You didn't?"

I paused my game of shark and tried to think, but my brain was fuzzy and it was difficult. "I don't know. I'm not really sure what made me say that."

"Your subconscious, perhaps?" She made her way over to the door. "It's probably just your imagination. The drugs. Lightning doesn't strike twice, right?"

"Who are you trying to convince?"

Janet reached out and took hold of the door knob. Twisting it hard, she pulled, allowing the door to swing wide open.

"No way," I whispered, pushing myself into a sitting position. Janet turned to look at me and started to say something, but I shook my head. "Run," I hissed. "Now!"

Janet nodded. Her face set with determination, she

scurried out into the hallway. Looking left, then right, she shot out of sight. The only sounds were those of her footsteps, fading further and further away, and my breathing, quickening with every beat of my heart. Through my medicinal haze, I strained to hear her, knowing that so long as I did, she was still okay.

Suddenly, there were loud shouts. Heavy footsteps. Some kind of alarm sounded. People began running past my room, the door still ajar from Janet's hasty departure. I watched as they sped past, aware of the fact that I was nothing more than a broken shadow, crumpled and lonely in the cold darkness. I hoped to remain invisible. Prayed that they would forget that I was in here. Perhaps, once my haziness cleared up a bit, I could make a run for it, too.

Instantly, my doorway plunged from light to dark, as a portly figure blocked my view of the hallway. I had the uneasy sensation that I'd met him somewhere before. As soon as he stepped into the light, I gasped. It couldn't be.

The man who had just entered my lonely, isolated cell was none other than Richard, Addison's longtime friend and ally with the Chicago PD.

We made eye contact and I felt my heart begin to race even faster, blood pounding in my ears. The medicine was making me light-headed. Woozily, I allowed myself to lay back down, splayed across the smooth cold concrete. Richard suddenly seemed unsure of himself, smoothing his hair and fidgeting with his shirt buttons. People were still racing through the hallway behind him. But Janet would make it out. She was smart. Resourceful. "Marian?" Richard asked quietly. "Why are you here?"

I narrowed my eyes and turned to face him. My speech was becoming more slurred with each passing second and my thoughts were fuzzy and untethered, but I wanted answers. "I could ask you the same thing," I breathed menacingly, though it probably sounded more like "Icouskyouasamethin" and my menacing gaze was probably more confused and tired.

"You knew I was involved in narcotics-" he started.

"Yeah, well not this involved," I snapped. "I'll have the police nail you on all kinds of charges."

This seemed to amuse him, which pissed me off, but my

brain wasn't understanding why. The haze. Oh, the haze. Why did people pay so much money for mind-altering drugs? They sucked. "Oh yeah?" he asked, crossing his arms in a jovial way. Much more jovial than he should have been, considering I could now testify that he was working with the enemy. "Like what, Moyer?"

"Like...drug trafficking," I stammered. "That's a charge. Kidnapping. Conspiracy. Grand...larceny."

Richard laughed long and low, his head tilting so far back that his Adam's apple strained for release. "Are you just listing off charges you watch on those cop shows of yours?"

"How do you know I watch cop shows?"

"You photograph crime scenes. Plus, Addison likes to talk."

"I'll kill her," I muttered. "And her little dog, too."

"I thought that last month, when I made you go on that date with James, you said I was the dog."

"You are the dog again! And a liar. And a...a thief. Of...goodness. A robber of good things in the world. You helped them steal my orgasms. I was this close," I whined, putting my thumb and index finger just inches apart.

"What?" he cried, blushing furiously. "Look, Marian, I don't think you-"

Just then, Gregson and his goateed thug burst through the door. "So it's true," Gregson murmured. "She did escape." He didn't seem incredibly surprised. It took him a few moments to notice Richard. "Dick," he sneered.

"Gregory," Richard sneered back.

"What are you doing here?"

Richard stood. "Just saw that the door was open. Thought someone should come in and make sure there wasn't any trouble."

There were a few tense moments of silence. Had we been in the Wild West, someone would have shot the other by now. "Well, there's no love lost between you two," I finally muttered. "You two part of rival outfits or something?"

Gregson chuckled, then grew serious again. "He wishes."

"Oh yeah," Richard responded sarcastically. "I so wish that I was on the screw up squad. Just wait 'til HE finds out that you let one of them escape. You're dead."

Gregson laughed and then reached deep into his pocket. Out of it, he drew a small silver pistol that gleamed in the soft light. "Not if he doesn't find out."

"Woah," Richard murmured, raising his hands defensively and stepping a little closer to me.

"What are you doing?" I screamed. "Don't come over here!"

"Don't shoot me," Richard pled.

"Don't shoot ME," I shouted. "And you!" I swatted at Richard from my vulnerable position on the floor. "Get away!"

"Yes, do kindly get the hell out of here," Gregson snapped at Richard. "Before I change my mind."

Richard hurried past Gregson, watching the pistol his entire escape. "Wait," I cried after him. "Take me with you!"

When he didn't return, Gregson turned to his man. "Were you the last one out of here?"

Goatee thought hard for a few moments. "I'm not sure," he answered dumbly. "I thought that I was out first." He frowned, trying hard to remember.

"No, you were last," Gregson barked. "The very last! You left the door unlocked! Again! Idiots! I'm dealing with idiots. You let that little tart escape."

Goatee's eyes widened in surprise and fear. It was hilarious, considering that he could have squashed Gregson like a bug. "I don't even have a key," Goatee stammered. "Why would you let me be last if I can't lock the door?"

"Let you?" Gregson cried. "It's called speaking up! 'Hey, boss! I don't have a key!'"

"But you told me to never speak first," Goatee murmured, contrite.

"Well, clearly there are some exceptions," Gregson spat. "Now get out of my sight. Before I decide to shoot you, too." Goatee shuffled quietly out of the room, eyes downcast, arms limply hanging by his sides. He seemed to hesitate briefly by the door, unsure of if he should speak up. "Well, you don't need to lock it now," Gregson growled over his shoulder. "I'm in here for heaven's sake."

"Sorry boss," and then the thug was gone.

"That wasn't very nice," I told Gregson. "You know as well as I do that you were the last one out of here."

Gregson's smile opened wide. "I know," he chuckled. "But that's always so much fun."

"Did you mean to leave the door unlocked?" I asked. My mouth seemed disconnected from the logic of my brain. Or perhaps the medicine had made me illogical. Either way, I was willing to ask and say things that I wouldn't normally.

Gregson's smile disappeared. "Of course not!" he snapped. Then he tapped his head. "Old brain. But if HE ever finds out it was my fault, I'm fish food. Better to have an alibi."

"Who is HE?" I asked, confused. "Can someone just answer that for me? I probably won't even remember. Oh, the room is spinning a bit."

"You'll probably find out who he is sooner or later," Gregson replied. "But for all of our sakes, let's hope that you don't."

We let the silence linger between us for a few moments. I found my thoughts, flighty as they were, wandering to Gregson and his past escapades. I wondered how long he had been involved in this whole mess. He didn't really strike me as the mob type, but I guess that goes to show that you never can tell, can you? I shuddered involuntarily, wondering if Gregson had ever actually killed anyone. Richard seemed to take him pretty seriously. Granted, Gregson didn't seem too keen on killing me. Maybe it was because I was a woman. Did gangsters live by the "women first/don't harm women" motif? Maybe I did stand a chance at getting out of here alive. If I could just avoid this

HE character.

"What's going to happen to her?" I asked quietly in the darkness, my thoughts slowly returning to Janet.

"There are a lot of places out there to hide," Gregson offered. Then with a frown he added, "But she wouldn't be the first one who tried to get away from him." The way that he'd said it had me hoping and praying that Janet would somehow be able to outsmart them. "And they have dogs," he added. "Really big dogs. Lots of teeth. And anger."

My stomach dropped as I remembered Shannon's beast that wanted to claw our faces off and eat them for breakfast. If Janet were to be caught, hopefully an actual person would be the one to do it.

"What happens if she's caught?" I asked.

Gregson shrugged. "Depends on who catches her. But best to not worry your pretty little self about that right now. How's your head?"

I yawned. "Fuzzy. And I'm kind of starting to feel sleepy."

Gregson began to back slowly out of the room. "I'll send someone to check on you in a few hours. Make sure you're still breathing."

"That's kind of you."

"Dead bodies begin to smell like rot quickly. Wouldn't want to be responsible for causing all that."

"Don't forget to lock the door," I mumbled, drifting away.

Gregson chuckled. "Oh, I don't think you'll be going anywhere."

Soon after Gregson stepped out, I passed out. If I was going to die in this hellhole, it would hopefully be in my sleep, which seemed like a rather peaceful way to go in the midst of such a violent storm.

When I awoke — who knew how long later — I felt as if I were in a fog. I didn't dare try to shake myself out of it but did notice a substantial reduction in the amount of pain I'd felt earlier. Slowly, carefully, I sat up and experienced no waves of nausea. Taking this as a good sign, I swiveled my head left and right. It appeared that the door to my room was closed. Locked, too, no doubt.

Janet was nowhere to be seen. I hoped that this meant she was well and quite far away, as opposed to lying facedown in some puddle surrounded by giant dogs.

Near the door sat a small tray with what looked to be toast and a glass of questionable looking water. I stood shakily and made my way over to it. Sniffing the water, I wrinkled my nose. It had a metallic quality to it and was rather cloudy. I debated for only a few seconds before pinching my nose and taking a quick gulp, cotton mouth winning out. Next, I went for the toast, which was cold and dry. God only knew how long that had been sitting there. Still, it was food. My stomach rumbled with hunger. Munching thoughtfully, I tried to piece together the last few hours.

Unfortunately, things weren't making a whole lot of sense. Sweet old Greg Gregson was a cold-blooded, drugwheeling killer. Addison's "inside guy" was actually a mole in the PD, working for The Man. Most confusing of all, Janet had managed to escape through sheer stupidity of the very people who had kidnapped us to begin with. An escape which had been prompted by Gregson, though seemingly accidentally. He'd admitted as much and I was clueless as to why. If someone came in and offered me release simply by letting them know how Janet had managed to escape, I'd sing like a canary.

Even though Janet and I hadn't found Riley, I had a sinking suspicion that she was close by. Gregson seemed to be the one thread that she, her mother and I had in common. Janet, I was sure, had been nothing more than collateral damage. Somewhere in the twisted web of reality was the truth, and it seemed as though I had nothing better to do than to sit down and try to figure it all out. Settling onto the floor, I leaned against the wall. My arms became riddled with goosebumps. The room was absolutely freezing, which I hadn't noticed until now.

Suddenly, the light above me began to flicker. I watched it warily, daring it to go out completely. It did. My prison was plunged into blackness. "Well this is just perfect," I muttered. "Perfect." I sighed, and laid my head against the wall, closing my eyes.

After a few moments, my heartbeat quickened as I realized that I was completely alone. Save for the giant spiders that were probably everywhere. I involuntarily squealed, scrunching myself into as small of a ball as possible. I hated spiders.

Taking a page from Addison's book of stress relief, I sucked in a huge shuddery breath and began to release it in a series of hoo's and ha's. Addison. Tears sprang to my eyes. I missed her. I missed my family. I missed James and Mika. Did they know that Janet and I were missing yet? Did Addison know that Richard was actually on the inside of this whole screwed up operation? If she didn't, would she find out before she became a victim, too? Was John okay? Had he been made aware of Rachel's involvement yet? Would Frank and my dad be able to work together with James and Mika to save us? And Rory. Was he still in Milwaukee? Had Carly shared the photos James had sent her? Was the entire nation on the lookout for Riley, Janet and I?

Just then, I heard the click of a key being entered into the door. When it opened, a sliver of light from the hall appeared. It disappeared almost as quickly when a silhouette stepped into the doorway. It was the thug with the eyeliner that had hauled Rachel in and out earlier. "We're going to play a little game," he said quietly. I narrowed my eyes. Who did he think he was? I wasn't playing anything.

My eyes wandered, taking in the cracks of light from the hall that danced around his bulging frame. I'd hoped to be able to squeeze past somehow and escape. Slide under his legs. Crawl over his bulk. That's when I noticed the large gun pointed at my liver. If he didn't manage to grab me as I scurried past, I had no doubt he'd shoot me.

"Since when do they give the help weapons?" I asked snidely.

Eyeliner ignored my question. "I haven't picked a name for our game just yet," he continued, "but it's going to go a little something like this. You tell me what you know and in return, I don't shoot you."

"Why do you need to know anything?" I bit back. "You're. The. Help." I wasn't sure why I was suddenly so emboldened but it was too late to call the words back. Besides, I didn't really want to.

"Gregson imagined that I could be a bit more...persuasive." He grinned, his eyes filling with a black emptiness that cut me down to my soul. Gregson might just use a gun to scare people, but this guy got off on murdering smart-asses like me.

"That doesn't sound like any fun," I responded, trying to keep my voice angry and level. "You get information for Gregson and what do I get out of the deal?"

"You don't get shot, dummy," he answered matter-of-factly.

"Well, surely there's something more enticing than that." I laughed, but it sounded strained — like a dying cat. "For all I know, you're just going to let me die in here, anyway. Shooting me is probably faster than starving to death, so I think I'll just keep my mouth shut." As if on cue, my stomach rumbled and I reached down to pat it. "Speaking of, I could really use a candy bar. My energy level is so low right now that I'm really not sure I could recall those details that you're wanting so badly."

"Oh, for heaven's sake!" I heard Gregson exclaim from the hallway. "Bruce, get out of my way."

"But, boss-" Eyeliner began. As he stepped aside, Gregson squeezed through the doorway.

"Nice to see you again," I smiled, relieved.

"You're feeling bold, Ms. Moyer," he responded with a snarl. "I was just sure that Bruce would be the key to your undoing."

I shrugged. "He's intimidating enough, I guess, but I kind of got the feeling he'd just kill me at the end of it all, anyway."

"Ah, so no motivation to really talk?" Gregson asked, nodding. I shrugged again, noncommittally. "Good, good," he nodded. Then turning to Bruce, he barked, "You can go now."

"But boss, I-"

"And give me your gun," Gregson added. Bruce sucked in a breath. He reminded me of a petulant child being told "no." "Now, Bruce," Gregson said, holding out his hand for the weapon.

"Fine," Bruce mumbled, slapping the gun into Gregson's hand. "Happy?"

"Quite," Gregson said with a smile. "You may go now, Bruce."

Bruce stalked out into the hallway. I couldn't help it. I began to giggle. It turned into laughter and eventually, tears were streaming down my face. Gregson stood amused, eventually asking, "What's so funny?"

When I had a handle on myself, I wiped the mirth from my cheeks. "This whole situation," I told him, finally.

Gregson nodded thoughtfully. "It is all quite the mess from in here," he said. "But I promise that for HIM, it's no laughing matter. HE will shoot you just as soon as he'll look at you. Most of them will. I need answers from you. Now. It's for your own good, really."

"I want answers, too," I shot back, no longer caring what danger I was putting myself in. I needed to know that everyone else I cared for would be safe. "I'd never have pegged you for a mid-level drug pusher," I started. "Or a mobster. Truth be told, you seemed to be way too nice for this line of business. At least, you were at some point. The Gregson that I knew was. Was that Grace's requirement? Bring home the bacon but just don't shoot anyone? Least of all, your neighbor?"

"Don't you dare say her name," Gregson snapped, pointing the gun towards my head. He shook his own head violently. "You know nothing," he hissed. With that, he pushed the door wide open and shoved me further into the dark room with one strong, bony arm.

I eyed Gregson's gun warily. I'd pushed the wrong button. Maybe he would kill me, after all. Or at the very least, shoot me. "How do I even know that the gun is loaded?" I asked.

Gregson looked down the hall to see if anyone was

coming, then swiftly pointed the gun into it and fired off a shot. He turned back to me and raised an eyebrow as if to say "satisfied?"

"Works for me," I said with a nod.

"Excellent," Gregson said, stepping into the room. His face was cast into darkness. "Quit sassing me. You're not off-limits just because we know one another. I have a job. If I don't do it, it's my life. And frankly, given the option between my own life and yours, I'll always pick mine," he growled.

"But you're so old-" I started.

"Shut up!" he screamed, causing my heart to skip a beat. I'd never heard him sound like that before. It was a mixture of terror and anger. "Now I start asking the questions," he fumed. "How did you figure all of this out?"

"Well, that's the thing," I answered. "I don't really have any of this figured out."

"What do you know?" His voice was dark. Dripping with maliciousness.

"I honestly have no idea," I countered.

"Stop it!" he cried, wagging the gun in my face, its shadow bouncing off the walls. "I want answers!"

"I really don't have any," I said with a shrug. "Really." I was terrified, but I refused to show it. "I'm honestly just as confused as you are right now." I paused. "Well, you're probably less confused because you don't have controlled substances of unknown origin in your system."

"You have no idea what I take," Gregson sneered. "I have

to have one of those weekly pill box counters for all the crap the doctors put into my system. High blood pressure. Heart medication. Fish oil. Vitamins."

"Sounds rough."

"It's terrible," he moaned. "Getting old ain't for sissies, girl."

"I believe you," I promised, pulling out the sympathy card. Maybe he'd stop pointing the gun at me if I sounded weak. Maybe then I could wriggle my way out of here.

Gregson wasn't having it. "Well, if you can't start there, let's backtrack. Just tell me how you came to be in this room."

"You know how I-"

"Quit sassing me. I said that I want your story from the beginning!" he roared.

"Okay, okay, geez," I said, crossing my arms. "Janet and I stumbled into your used bookstore in-"

"No!" Gregson yelled. "Don't you understand English? From the beginning. How did you get involved in all of this in the first place? Why did you even come to visit me? Was it that stupid sister-in-law of yours? Did she tell you-"

"She didn't say anything," I cut him off. "You kidnapped my niece," I felt the words slip out involuntarily. It was a gamble because I actually had no real evidence that he had taken Riley. She could still be in danger somewhere totally outside of this hellhole and I could do nothing to save her. Still, if I could get him to admit she was nearby, I might be able to add another piece to the puzzle I was trying to piece together before Gregson could. His bushy eyebrows shot up in surprise but he masked his emotion quickly. "I know she's here," I went on.

"Do you?" he asked slowly.

I nodded. "And I'll just bet that you were the one who wrote up those ransom notes," I continued. This was also just a guess. Gregson glared at me but didn't speak, so I continued. "The ransom amount you requested was pretty random. Is that some rough estimate of your lifetime rent over at the assisted living- er- retirement facility that you need?"

Gregson sneered. I swallowed hard. I'd overstepped the boundary somewhere. Probably by mistakenly referring to his new home as assisted living. Suddenly, through the thick fog still enveloping my brain, it came to me. Rachel had all but refused to give us specifics related to Riley's kidnapping. Hell, she hadn't even been willing to tell us directly that Gregson was involved. He'd incriminated himself all on his own. Rachel had probably been threatened to keep her mouth shut about the whole operation. My stomach rolled with contempt. How had she even gotten involved with these idiots in the first place?

Gregson continued to stare at me, gun raised, unblinking. He was waiting for me to continue. Suddenly, it occurred to me. He was trying to figure out how much I knew of his plot. Which told me that there was an endgame, even if we didn't know what it was. He was wondering if I was still useful.

This whole thing was probably never about kidnapping Riley. But for whatever reason, someone, somewhere, had deviated from the real plan and thrown a wrench into everything. A wrench Gregson was trying hard to rip free before he got tossed in jail.

The plan was salvageable. I wasn't sure if it involved killing those of us that knew about it, but Gregson didn't seem to have cold-blooded murder on his agenda, assuming he could avoid it. Whoever "he" was could, but perhaps, if I was honest with Gregson, I'd gain an ally and he'd let us live. It was the only chance I really had right now.

"How is Don?" Gregson asked suddenly.

"My dad?" I asked. "Fine," I responded warily. "Why?"

Gregson chuckled. "Just making conversation. You do look so much like him when you're weighing things in your mind, Marian. I hope you take that as a compliment. Anyway, please go on with what you know."

I figured that it couldn't hurt to share everything. Perhaps by sharing everything that I knew, Gregson would inadvertently offer me a few clues that could help me make sense of some things.

I started from the beginning. The call from my parents, driving to see them, the ransom that made us think it was a debt owed, possibly for something illegal, the hidden bank accounts that we'd found, the search for my niece, Gregson's lead that led us to the bookstore, Ernie's idiocy, the car accident, "And you know the rest better than I do," I finished.

"Interesting," Gregson mused. He seemed to take his sweet time, drinking in my story slowly like you would a good scotch. He let it consume him, fill him. He closed his eyes, pleasured by the taste of it.

"It's a weird world," I admitted. "But you can see that I'm missing quite a few bits and pieces of the story."

"You seem to know enough to pin things together if you tried," he told me, opening one eye. "In fact, I should just shoot you right now before you have the opportunity." I swallowed, recalling the time that Barry had cornered me in my apartment with a gun. He'd said something eerily similar. Funny how I kept getting myself into these messes.

Gregson grinned and looked lovingly at the gun before dropping it down to his side. "But I think I'll just leave you before I do something stupid."

"Well, wait," I urged, emboldened by my stroke of luck. "I've upheld my end of the bargain. I've told you everything that I know."

"I suppose that means that you want a few answers yourself now, right?" Gregson asked. I weighed my opportunity to run. He'd already proven that the gun held bullets. It was probably best to stay put. Instead, I waited for him to continue. Perhaps he'd say something I could use. He eyed me long and hard, like a hawk studying a field mouse. Despite the medicinal fog that lingered around my brain, I felt as though he was up to something. I simply wasn't sure as to what. "You've already figured out that none of this is about Riley," he went on.

My heart began to hammer and I could feel my breath becoming slightly more rapid. I'd been right. Riley was a pawn. But now that they had her, what would they do with her? "So what was it about?" I asked him. "Why me? Why Marian Moyer?"

Gregson softened. When he looked at me, I knew that a million memories from my childhood were running through his mind. Almost as quickly, he snapped, raising the gun again and pointing it directly at my face. He couldn't afford to be soft in his line of business and he was onto my game. I raised my hands in an act of defense, even though I knew it wouldn't do me any good if he decided to shoot.

Gregson was close to 80. Maybe he didn't have as great of a shot as he'd had in his younger years when he first got into the business, but I wasn't going to be the one to test that theory with some stupid escape attempt. "Don't do that," he said angrily, shaking the gun. "Don't you do that to me right now."

"But I didn't-" I started.

"Shut up," he said lowly.

I took a deep breath. "Fine," I said, lowering my hand. "Fine, I understand that you can't be my friend in here. What can you give me, then?" I asked, leaning towards him curiously.

Gregson seemed to relax a bit. "I can't really give you anything, Marian," he responded. "But I need you to use your brain. That brain that I know you have." I stared at him, confused. What the hell did all of that mean? "Is the ransom amount really so random?" he asked, continuing on quietly. "Think, Marian. Think really hard."

"It's rather difficult to do right now," I muttered. "My head is in a bit of a fog."

"Ah, yes. The pills." Gregson frowned and lowered the gun again. I breathed a sigh of relief. When he began to step out of the room, I started towards him but he raised the gun again, making me stop short. "You already have all of the information you need," he whispered.

"Is she here?" I asked him. "Did you take her? Is she okay? Is Riley alive?"

"She's alive," he promised.

"Let me see her. Please."

Gregson thought about this for a moment before he wagged a finger. "Wait right here." With that, he closed the door behind him and I heard the deadbolt lock into place.

"Wait!" I screamed, lunging for the door. The sudden movement caused a sharp pain in my head. I gripped my skull and nearly knelt to the floor with a small scream of pain and frustration. I was still groggy but the pills were definitely starting to wear off. God only knew how long it would be until I would receive more. I started to sweat, heavy cold beads, as I squatted there, holding myself in a ball, rocking back and forth. I felt like a crazy person. Maybe I was going crazy.

A few minutes later, I heard the deadbolt click again and Gregson entered with his gun. When he saw me, however, he didn't raise it, deciding that I wasn't much of a threat. "You can see Riley," he began, and my heart leapt with joy. She really was here. She was alive. Gregson would let me see her! "But first, you have to exercise those criminal investigation chops."

I stared at him dumbfounded. "How? What do you mean?"

Gregson shifted and looked down the hallway before turning back to me. In a low whisper he said, "You're focused on the wrong thing."

"I shouldn't be focused on trying to find my niece?" I asked him angrily, dropping my hands to the cold, hard ground and pushing myself to my feet. "Tell me, what should I be focused on in this whole mess?"

"I didn't say any of that," Gregson snapped easily. "Quit being so hot-headed and focus, Moyer."

"I am so confused," I said desperately. "I don't know what you want from me."

"Figure it out," Gregson cried. "For Riley's sake."

With that, he stepped back and slammed the door shut, once again locking the deadbolt. This time, I didn't even make a move for the door. My head was beginning to pound. I didn't have much time to figure out Gregson's riddles before my brain was rendered useless by pain. Knowing this, I slowly made my way down to the floor, where I laid down on the smooth, cool concrete. It felt good against my hot skin, which was prickling with sweat.

Once my body had cooled and the pounding in my head

had diminished to a dull drumming, I tried to think. Gregson told me that I was focusing on all of the wrong things. What had we been talking about just before all of that? I squinted into the darkness, willing myself to remember. He'd wanted to know everything. What had he meant that I was focused on the wrong thing?

Suddenly a light bulb went off in my head, just as the dingy light bulb in my room flickered back on. "The ransom note," I said aloud to no one in particular. That was odd. Was Gregson telling me that we shouldn't be focused on the ransom note? I was beginning to get the feeling that he'd been in on Riley's kidnapping, but I didn't understand how that made the ransom any less important. I wasn't entirely sure how he'd helped abduct her, as Riley could have easily escaped him. Someone else had to have been involved. Richard, perhaps. That didn't really fit, though. Surely someone would have noticed Richard. A stranger of his appearance in a very small town would have been memorable to someone in the hours leading up to Riley's disappearance.

I sighed and slowly rolled from my stomach to my back. My head began to hammer again and I closed my eyes tightly, begging the pain to subside just a little bit longer. When it did, I tried hard to think again. I didn't have much longer before my brain was going to be completely useless. In that moment, I felt tears spring to my eyes. I thought of Riley, my parents, my brother, my friends who had come so far to help us find my niece. Did they have any idea where she was? Perhaps Janet had somehow gotten word home and they were on their way. Maybe the Chicago PD was going to burst in at any moment and rescue me. It's not like I was really the damsel in distress type. I take pride in being able to hang my own picture frames and unclog my own sink. Still, there were always those rare occasions when you just needed a helping hand, and if this instance didn't qualify, I wasn't sure what did. "Focus," I snapped to myself, angrily. "No pity parties."

Gregson told me I was focused on the wrong thing. The ransom seemed the likely perpetrator. Originally, we'd thought that the amount was an amount owed for some horrible illegal debt. That's what had originally led us to the bank accounts. Was it not owed? The amount could be for drugs that Rachel had sold but didn't hand over the money for. That made sense, but it didn't feel right in my gut. Did the ransom have nothing to do with the drug trafficking? That would be a real loop.

I pondered over this for a few seconds. It felt good. I dropped the possibility that the ransom amount was owed for drugs. Besides, all of that would mean that Rachel would have had to have sold them in the first place. I was pretty sure that Rachel didn't know the first thing about actually selling narcotics, though moving them was totally different. Heck, I didn't know the first thing about selling narcotics and I worked with the police. I suppose she could have dumped them somewhere so that they couldn't be used but that just sounded plain stupid. Why would anyone simply get rid of a bunch of valuable drugs if it meant putting their life at risk for nothing?

I sighed. My headache was increasing with each passing moment. If the ransom had nothing to do with an amount owed, what could it possibly have to do with? Maybe if I could just figure that out, I'd be well on my way to solving this whole nightmare. "Probably just in time to be rescued because everyone else had it all figured out hours ago," I mumbled. Granted, they all had a few hours on me. I'd been asleep for who knew how long.

I allowed my thoughts to stray from crime solving back to my niece. I could picture her adorable freckled face, her other physical features that were so strikingly like her mother's. Her sharp wit. Her loud-mouthed attitude. Though it was still winter, I found my thoughts straying to her birthday coming up that next June. I had promised to take her to the Wisconsin Dells. Thirteen was a big year. It deserved something special. Would I ever see Riley again? Would we be able to go on that trip I'd promised her, her last birthday? Was she thinking about it, too, wondering if I'd save her in time?

I felt my heart spring to my throat with realization, though I wasn't entirely sure why. I went back through my thoughts. Find Riley. Wisconsin Dells. Birthday. June. "Six," I whispered. Grimacing against the pain, I rolled back onto my stomach and slowly pushed myself to my knees. The nausea was back. My stomach pitched but I ignored it as I climbed to my feet. Desperately, I started looking around the room for a security camera, hoping someone would pay attention to the fact that I had something to say. When I couldn't find one, I lurched towards the door and began pounding against it. My head protested but I didn't care. "Six Twenty-Three!" I screamed. "It's Riley's birthday! June 23rd is her birthday!" Gregson was right. Our group had been so convinced that the ransom was for some amount of money owed, when that was clearly far from the truth. Still, it had led us to Rachel's hidden bank accounts which had led us to Gregson and to the bookstore and eventually here, even if it was all one big happy accident.

Just then, I heard the deadbolt click out of place. I went to grab for the knob but thought the better of it and took a step away from the door. For all I knew, they had a bazooka on the other side.

The door swung open and I saw two skinny shadows. One was Gregson, with his gun buried deep into the back of the shadow in front of him. "Riley?" I whispered.

"Aunt Em?" came her quiet, hesitant voice.

With a sob, we both launched ourselves into the other's arms.

I stroked Riley's hair with my left hand. Through my tears, I gently ran my right hand over her shoulders, her arms, her back and her stomach, searching for any signs of injury or abuse. "Are you okay?" I asked her over and over.

"I'm okay," she kept repeating back to me, nodding into my shoulder.

I'm not sure how long we stood there. I also didn't realize that Gregson stood with his gun pointed towards us the whole time. "That's sweet," he sighed when our tears of happiness had finally subsided.

"Could you put that thing down?" I snapped at him, pointing towards the gun. "She's been through enough, don't you think?"

Gregson smiled at me but didn't lower his gun. "I brought you something else," he told me slowly.

Reaching into his pants pocket he removed two small, white pills. "More pain medicine?" I asked him. He nodded. "I can't. I'll fall asleep again."

He shrugged and slowly went to set the pills on the floor by the door. "Suit yourself. Still have that water I gave you earlier?"

I wrinkled my nose and glanced at the cloudy half glass still sitting on the tray.

"Good," he said with a curt nod.

"It's not exactly-" I started.

"You're lucky you're getting hospitality at all," Gregson cut me off. "In case you haven't noticed, you're not exactly in a room at the Ritz."

"Believe me, I've noticed," I told him dryly. He smiled wryly and I took this to mean that he was in a somewhat good mood, so I decided to press him for what I could. "Now what?" I asked.

"What do you mean?" he asked.

"Well, I solved the mystery," I insisted. "The ransom was for nothing, it was just to throw us off. You probably didn't even mean to kidnap Riley. You probably didn't mean for any of us to be here." Gregson said nothing but continued to aim the gun at us. Riley clung to my waist, her head buried in my shoulder. "So if that's it, why don't you just let us go? You don't need us. It was a mistake. We'll go. We won't tell anyone about anything we've seen. Let's just forget that any of this ever happened."

Gregson laughed, a cold hollow sound. "You're right, I don't need you." With those words, he removed the safety from the gun. "In fact, it's too bad I'm not in charge because I trust you, Marian. I trust that you wouldn't tell a soul," Gregson said as he took a deep, shuddery breath. "But he doesn't. He doesn't trust anyone. Try to escape, I'll shoot you. I told you. Me or you- I'll always pick me."

Confused, I started to ask him what he'd meant, but the door was already closing. "Wait!" I cried, letting go of

Riley and moving towards the door. I managed to grab the handle and tug hard, but it was too late. The deadbolt had just clicked into place. "Damn it!" I screamed, slamming my fist hard into the door. "Yeow!" I cried, shaking my hand and hopping from foot to foot.

Whimpering, I slid to the floor. After the pain had subsided a bit, I looked up to Riley and smiled tightly. "What do we do now?" she asked, coming over to sit next to me.

I slid my arm around her shoulder and pulled her close. "I have no idea," I told her quietly. Kissing the top of her head, I added, "But I'm going to figure that out."

One thing that quickly became obvious was that I wasn't going to be getting Riley and myself out of anywhere given the amount of pain I was in. I had no choice but to take the pills that Gregson had offered. I found myself hoping that somehow, this round wouldn't zonk me out as readily as the last one had, even though I realized how foolish that probably was.

Thankfully, consciousness came just as quickly as sleep had. When I awoke, I was sitting up, asleep against the door to our prison. Riley herself was strewn across my lap, snoring quietly, a small line of drool dried to her chin. Smiling, I lovingly pushed back her stick straight blond hair, causing her to snort and stir. A few seconds later, she blinked awake and stretched her arms wide. "What time is it?" she asked.

"No idea," I admitted. "But I don't think it's been more than about a few hours. Any idea what time it was when they brought you in?"

Riley shook her head. I had the odd feeling like I always get in Vegas. Addison and I had gone there with a bunch of friends a few years ago, and again last year by ourselves. While neither of us were big gamblers, it was alarming how easily a casino can suck you in. With no clocks and no windows, you don't know if you've been sitting at a slot machine for ten minutes or three hours. The feeling is enough to drive someone mad.

Between the crash, the two rounds of pills and getting Riley back, I suspected that I had been off the radar for at least 12 to 15 hours. It would be long enough that, even if Janet hadn't been able to find help, everyone back home would know something was wrong. They might even be searching for us in the city right now. On the other hand, it wasn't long enough to have filed a missing person's report, so as far as the local police were concerned, I wasn't actually missing yet. However, Riley definitely was and I could only hope that her face was receiving some national coverage.

I tried hard to shake the medicinal fog that surrounded my brain. The pain had reduced substantially. Nonetheless, I didn't feel nearly as sharp as I needed to be in order to find Riley and I a way out. "There are so many things about this situation that just don't fit," I said, thinking aloud. Riley looked up at me curiously. "I guess first things first, though," I said to her. "Who kidnapped you? I know Gregson couldn't have acted alone. You'd have totally been able to take him."

Riley grinned a toothy smile and shook her head. She was 12 going on 30, but appeared so much younger in that moment. I felt an angry fire begin to burn in my belly. It was beyond me who could possibly kidnap a child. "Mr. Gregson wasn't even there," Riley answered.

"Can you tell me what you remember?" I asked.

She nodded. As it turned out, she had been on her way to my mom and dad's house when she was abducted. How she had gotten out of the house remains a mystery. My brother cut down the tree outside her window when she was younger. She used to shimmy down its trunk. Now that the tree was no longer there, it was a mystery to all of us, her parents included, how she still managed to sneak out of the house. When I interrupted her story to ask, she just gave me a sly smile and continued. She'd been about halfway to Grandma and Pop Pop's when she heard a car crunching through the snow behind her. When she turned to look, she noticed that whoever it was had very tinted windows and out-of-state plates. She'd started to speed up and so did the car. Eventually, two men she didn't recognize got out and dragged her kicking and screaming into the backseat. The sidewalks had been well shoveled, so she'd left behind no signs of struggle. Before they'd even driven out of town, someone had put a bag over her head. She'd felt a slight prick in her arm.

Next thing she knew, she had woken up in a room not so different from the one we were in now. Gregson had seemed surprised by her arrival but kind to her, and for that I was grateful. She'd had food, water and even a mattress. Not that you could get much sleep, given the situation. Every time the door opened, she confessed she'd been terrified that it was someone coming to drag her away and that she'd never see us again. She had no idea where she was or if she'd ever be released. On top of that, she had no idea why she'd been kidnapped in the first place. The girl was going to need therapy and I personally would be making these jerks pay for it.

"Were your parents still at home when you were kidnapped?"

Riley nodded and her eyes started to fill with tears. "They must be so angry that I snuck out of the house. If I hadn't, none of this ever would have happened." With that, her small body became wracked with sobs.

Horrified, I pulled her tightly to my chest. "Why would you even think that? They've been so worried about you."

"I just mess everything up," she sniffled, wiping her nose on her sleeve. "I try to be good, I really do. It's hard. And I'm the only one, so they see everything. You're so lucky that you had a big brother!"

"Why were you grounded?" I asked her gently, ignoring the rest of her plight. Having an older brother had been no picnic. Sure we got along...now. Growing up, however, I'd had to share everything. Grass is always greener as they say.

Her cheeks reddened slightly and she looked down at her fingernails. "Grades," she answered in a nearly inaudible whisper. "They were released for winter quarter."

"Not so great, huh?"

Riley shook her head and smiled wryly. "Let's just say I'm not in danger of making Honor Roll."

I chuckled and pulled her close for another hug. "I'm not going to tell you that grades aren't important, kiddo," I murmured into her hair. "But they're not nearly as important as your safety and well being. The circumstances that led to you being brought here were out of your control. Plus, I'm almost 30 and I've never once had to use the Pythagorean Theorem."

"The what?"

"Forget it."

Riley seemed to think hard for a few moments. Finally, she asked, "Aunt Em? Do you think I was kidnapped because of, er- what does Grandpop call it? Car moo?"

"Karma," I corrected, giggling.

"Yeah, that," she continued. "It's like fate or something."

"Sort of," I agreed. "It's the idea that what you did comes back to you. So good things will bring you good, and bad things will bring you bad."

"And running away so many times might have finally caught up with me," Riley admitted.

I smiled. "So when we get you out of here, you promise not to sneak out any more?" Riley grinned and shrugged, wiping her tear-stained cheeks with her palms. "I thought as much," I laughed, pinching her arm. Talking to Riley had helped me to shake off the rest of my sleep. My brain was still clouded by medicine but I was gaining confidence in my ability to get us out before the pain came back in full force. "I need your help," I told her quietly.

Eagerly, Riley sat back on her heels and smoothed her hair behind her ears. "Anything," she promised. She meant it. It was one thing I admired about the kid. She had real moxie.

"I need you to help me think. Since we can't get out of here-" I turned and once again tried to tug the door. It was still locked tight. "Since we can't get out of here," I repeated with a sigh, "we need to figure out how we ended up here in the first place. Maybe that'll give us some kind of clue."

"So what can I do?" Riley asked, confused. "I don't know why I'm here. You told Gregson you thought it was an accident."

I smiled. "That's true, I do think that. But you can start throwing out ideas. Anything that seemed weird or different in the days before your kidnapping. Anything that someone has said while you've been here that gave you a funny feeling. Even if it sounds silly."

Riley closed her eyes tightly while she searched her memories. After a few minutes, they opened wide. "We got a lot of weird phone calls at the house recently," she told me, her eyes growing dark with the memories.

"Like...really weird."

"What do you mean?"

"Well-" Riley said, trying to think of a way to explain. "The phone never really rings. We're not like, a cool family or anything. It's only ever Kelsey asking if I can come over. Or Grandma and Grandpop."

I nodded encouragingly. "Go on."

Riley took a deep breath and continued. "But last week, someone kept calling the house and hanging up. A few times someone asked for mom. In a funny voice. Like it wasn't really theirs."

"How could you tell it wasn't theirs?"

"It sounded like this," Riley said, forcing her words to become deep but airy.

"Interesting."

Riley paused for a moment as she realized something. "No one ever asked for dad, though. Just mom. Do you think that's an important thing to know?"

I nodded again. "I think that it is," I told her, my mind flashing to Rachel's secret bank accounts. "Did anyone ever ask if you were home by yourself?"

Riley shook her head and rolled her eyes. "I would have lied anyway. You learn that in, like, first grade. Duh."

"Kids still say "duh"?"

"Duh."

"Fair enough," I laughed. "What about while you have been here? Does anything seem weird?"

Riley thought hard again but seemed to come up empty.

"I guess just that Mr. Gregson has been kind of strange."

"How so?"

"Well," Riley pondered "like he's being really, really nice." She made a face to suggest that this wasn't his usual demeanor when she came in contact with him. Strange considering I'd grown up thinking that he was an incredibly kind man. "And when someone would be mean, like tell me to shut up or stop crying, he'd come in and make them leave."

How did you explain to a 12 year old that her kidnapper probably didn't even mean to kidnap her in the first place? Hell, he didn't seem to want any of us stuck in here, even though I didn't doubt he'd kill us if he absolutely had no other alternative. I could only guess that it had something to do with the HIM everyone around here kept mentioning. "Riley, this next question is really important," I told her. "Did Gregson ever offer to help you to get out of the building?"

"No, nothing like that" she answered quickly. When I stared at her with a raised eyebrow, she hurriedly continued. "Well, so, when he brought me here, he told me he wanted to help. We were walking down the hallway but when we turned the corner, it looked like someone was standing at the end of it. Gregson got mad all of a sudden, pulled out a gun and pointed it at me, saying that I'd better start minding him. I didn't know what he meant. He'd asked me to follow him in the first place. Anyway, I heard you yelling and I asked him if I could see you. That's when he brought me in here." She thought for a few seconds. "I feel like he was bringing me down here anyway." She shrugged. "I dunno. Probably sounds dumb."

"No, not dumb," I assured her quickly. "Where was the room where you were, in relation to where we are now?"

Riley pointed to the left. "Down that way."

"Did you see who was standing at the end of the hallway? The person that made Gregson start acting funny?" It was possible that this was the key — that Riley was about to reveal who HE was. I waited while she scrunched her eyes closed and thought.

"Well," she finally answered, "I didn't see a face, if that's what you mean. But his body reminded me of Santa's. Even though, ya know, Santa isn't real or anything."

"Richard?" I asked, wrinkling my nose in confusion.

"Who?" Riley asked.

"Was it a man?" I continued. "Did he have a beard?"

"I think it was a man," she told me, obviously unsure. "I couldn't see a face at all. I don't know if he- she- um- I don't know if they had a beard. I could just see an outline. You know." She held her arms out by her sides and briefly ballooned her cheeks to demonstrate someone of a much heavier weight than she was.

"But Gregson knew who it was immediately," I said as Riley's breath whooshed out. It was not a question. "And it scared him enough to make him pretend he had control over you with his gun."

Riley nodded. "I think so. I mean, I guess. I don't really

know what's going on Aunt Em." I was about to ask her about how long the hallway was and if she'd been able to see any kind of exit, when I heard a key enter the door lock. Quickly, Riley and I scuttled to our feet, curious to see who would be coming in. Maybe we were finally being sprung. Perhaps this entire nightmare was ending just as strangely and suddenly as it had begun.

I couldn't have been more wrong.

"Janet," I whispered as soon as the door swung open. She was passed out in the arms of Shannon, the giant bald man from the bookstore, who at least had the decency to look apologetic. Thankfully, he was without his mangy fanged mutt. "What the hell happened to her?" I asked him angrily.

"I heard that you were in here, too," he told me, ignoring my question. I'd show him. I marched over to try to pull her from his hands, but he easily pushed me away. "Don't try anything stupid," he told me, gently setting Janet on the ground. He hesitated just before he closed the door behind himself, locking it. "She should be awake soon. She's safer in here. With you."

"Why does everyone keep saying that we're safer in here?" I yelled after him. "We're safer out of here. Free! Like birds!" I flapped my arms briefly to demonstrate, but I'm not sure if he was able to see or hear my full display. It didn't really matter. I hurried to Janet's side and Riley came over to kneel down next to me.

"Who is Janet?" she asked quietly.

"My very good friend. She came all the way from Florida to help us find you," I answered. "She's a cop."

"She's with the police?"

"Not locally, but yes."

"She came just for me?"

"You think she left 80 degrees and a beach for sub-zero and snow for just me?" I let out a loud, short laugh. "You have a lot of people that love you, kiddo. Even people you've never met." I chucked her gently under the chin.

Riley gently picked up Janet's hand and began to stroke it. "Do you think she can feel that?" she asked me.

In response, Janet moaned. I leaned over her and gently patted her cheek. "Wake up," I whispered urgently. "Janet, it's Marian. Please wake up."

"Are we in the hospital?" she grunted, not bothering to open her eyes. "Are we free?"

"No," I admitted dully, sitting back on my heels.

Janet opened one eye and took a quick look around the room. "Damn," she muttered.

"Language!" I scolded. "Children are present."

Janet opened both eyes and immediately realized that the person holding her hand wasn't me, but a miniature version of Rachel. "Are you Riley?" she breathed. When Riley nodded shyly, Janet sat up to give her a hug. "I'm so glad you're okay!" she cried. "We were looking everywhere for you."

"Janet, what happened?" I asked as she kept Riley pulled fiercely to her chest. "After you got out of here, where did you go? Did you find help? Is anyone coming for us?"

Janet just shook her head and let a small moan of embarrassment escape her lips. Riley, from her position, patted Janet awkwardly on the back to soothe her. "We're in the middle of nowhere," Janet told me, devastated. "There wasn't a car I could hotwire, there wasn't a person other than all of these bodyguards that look exactly the same, save for small personal details. Speaking of, what's up with that muscle head with the goatee? I mean, seriously, dude. Did Gregson employ a couple of quadruplets or something? Anyway, I was hiding when that stupid dog from earlier today almost ripped my throat out. Snuck up behind me. I had no idea it was capable of being so quiet." She shuddered, releasing Riley's head from her iron grip.

I was horrified and immediately leaned forward to pat her down for injuries. "How did you get out of that one?" Janet's shirt was much dirtier than it had been before she escaped and it looked like a chunk had been ripped away by something sharp. Teeth, perhaps? Her undershirt, also dirty, remained fully intact. Her dress slacks were torn and dirty and one of her hands had a small cut across the palm.

Janet shrugged and pulled her hand away to inspect it. "That Shannon guy. I started to run and the dog was gaining on me. Sliced my hand on something as I went. Caught my shirt on these wooden crates that are everywhere out there, but just kept going. I could feel the thing nipping at my ankles. I was trying to kick it in the face. I turned a corner and ran smack into Shannon's chest. He's totally ripped by the way- it's not just his arms. I felt like I'd hit a brick wall."

"Keep going," I encouraged.

"Oh, sorry," Janet said quickly, shaking off thoughts of Shannon's solid muscles. "So anyway, I run into Shannon and he just lifts me up and puts me behind him. The dog sees him and instantly freezes. Shannon told me I had to follow him back here. The dog followed us, growling the whole way. I didn't really have a choice."

"When did you pass out?"

"I didn't pass out," she said defensively, crossing her arms. "Shannon stashed me in some room down the hall. Then the guy with the goatee comes in and starts trying to get fresh. Tells me he knows I want it. Tells me no one is going to find out." My eyes widened and Riley's sparked with interest. I immediately clamped my hands over her ears as Janet continued, completely oblivious to the fact that there was a pre-teen in the room. "So I tell him he's right. Call him Baby, real sweet. He reaches for my zipper and, bam," she jerks her hand in and upward motion, "I shove his nose back into his skull and knee him in the nads."

One of my hands slipped from Riley's ear to cover my mouth. "Holy crap."

"So he starts screaming and then the one with the earrings and the eyeliner comes in and knocks me into the wall." She brushed back her hair to reveal an ugly bruise I hadn't noticed earlier. "That's the last thing I remember."

"I can't believe you did that. I can't believe you're okay. You're okay?"

"I'm okay."

I took a deep breath. "Okay." Desolation began to set in. I removed my other hand from Riley's ear. "So you've pretty much been in here the whole time we thought you were out finding help."

She shook her head sadly. "Sorry, Em." She grinned. "I can't believe you didn't hear him screaming, though. He was cussing pretty loudly. This," she pointed to her her bruise, "was so worth it."

"Have you seen Rachel again?" I asked, not thinking. I'd forgotten Riley was there, too.

She perked up instantly. "Mom's here?"

Janet shot me a concerned look. "I haven't seen her," she told me. Turning to Riley, she continued, "But I'm sure she's around here somewhere." She looked at me again. We were both thinking the same thing. Hopefully, when we did see Rachel again, she'd be alive. For Riley's sake.

Slowly, Janet pushed herself off the floor and stood, dusting off the seat of her pants. As she bent forward, a loud ripping sound sliced through the room. "Great," she muttered, patting her bum where the huge opening appeared, revealing her pink undies. "Of all the places."

Walking over to the door, Janet tugged at the handle, hoping for a third miracle. "Locked tight," she sighed when it didn't budge.

"Gregson blamed your escape on one of his henchmen," I giggled. "It was pretty funny."

Janet smiled as Riley released an audible sigh. "Anything

else happen while I was out?" Janet asked, moving back to my side.

"Not much," I assured her. "Although, it would seem that Richard is actually working from the inside, as opposed to working for the police. Another dirty cop." I shook my head in disgust. "How many more do you think there are?"

"THE Richard?" Janet asked. She knew all about Barry as well as the players involved in that whole fiasco.

"That's the one," I murmured.

"Who is Richard?" Riley hissed.

"Well, wait, if he's on the force, maybe he's just a mole," Janet said, ignoring Riley.

"Exactly," I told her. "A big, fat rat bastard working to bring down the Chicago police."

"Who is Richard?" Riley tried again.

"No, Marian, what if he's acting as a mole for this entire operation?" Janet asked, her eyes lit up with excitement. "FOR the police? What if he can help us get out of here?"

I felt my eyes nearly bug out of their sockets. "Holy crap!" I whispered. "How did I miss that?"

"You have a severe head injury," Janet supplied. "I think that you can be afforded a slip here and there." I motioned to her head wound but she shrugged. "A scratch."

Riley crossed her arms and stared at both of us. With an angry scowl she cried out, "Who's Richard? What is going on?"

I took her by the shoulders and squatted so that we were eye level. "I don't have time to explain right now," I told her hurriedly. The pain in my head was mild but I could tell that it was starting to return. We had to make a move before that happened or we'd be forced to wait for hours until I was given more pills and slept them off. "But I think we might be able to get out of here. Soon. I need you to do whatever Janet or I tell you to do. No one else. Understood?" Riley's eyes widened and she nodded in agreement. I nodded back. "Good."

Standing upright and dropping my arms, I again turned to Janet. "Who do you suppose is in charge of this whole thing? Gregson and Richard both mentioned "him," so we know it isn't either one of them."

Janet wrinkled her nose. "Ernie? Shannon?" she guessed.

I rolled my eyes. "Does Ernie really seem like the type to run a drug ring under wraps?"

"You never know," she said shrugging. "Sometimes it's the quiet ones."

I began to laugh. It wasn't even all that funny, but the entire situation was so whacked out and ridiculous, that I just couldn't help it. After a few seconds, Janet began to laugh, too. Riley joined in. I couldn't blame her. Janet's laugh was infectious and only made me laugh harder.

I'm not sure how long we were cracking up but, somewhere above the noise, my ears picked up on a sharp click. Abruptly, I stopped giggling and turned to face the door. The others did the same.

"Mom!" Riley screamed, both shocked and excited as the

door swung wide open. As she turned to run into her mother's arms, however, a loud shot rang out. The unmistakable sound of a gun. Rachel pitched forward, her mouth a round "O" of surprise. Eyes blank. Blood. Chaos.

"Mom!" Riley's terrified scream echoed off the walls of our dark prison. Everything seemed to slow down. I saw Riley racing towards Rachel out of the corner of my eye. As Rachel fell forward, blood spattered across her white, delicate top, Janet launched forward. She caught Rachel in her arms, just before they both hit the ground. Meanwhile, I made a grab for Riley and pulled her into my body. Wrapping her in my arms, I forced us to turn away from the grisly scene unfolding before our eyes.

"What the-" I heard Janet ask, confused. Daring to turn around, I saw a large round body lying face down in the hallway. The shirt was slightly too short and the pants were just a little too tight. I strained to see facial features, but they were covered in blood. Meanwhile, Janet's hands were flying across Rachel's back, feeling for an entry wound. "There's no bullet. I can't find the bullet," she was calling to me. She hadn't even noticed the body out in the hallway.

"I'm not hit," Rachel cried, pushing herself off Janet.

"He was," I said nodding towards the hallway. Riley was squirming hard in my grasp. I released her and she tripped over me, falling to her knees. Uncaring, she crawled the rest of the way across the floor and into her mother's arms.

"Mama," she kept crying over and over, as tears rushed down her face.

"I'm sorry, baby. I'm so sorry," Rachel was crooning into Riley's ear.

Janet stood and turned to me, dumbfounded. "Who is that?" she hissed.

"It's Ernie," Rachel told us over Riley's head.

My stomach dropped. I knew he'd looked familiar. "Ernie from the bookstore?" I asked her quietly.

Rachel nodded and hugged Riley even tighter. "He just came in and grabbed me. Said we had somewhere to be. He had a gun, so I did what he said. I haven't made it this far only to get shot. He unlocked the door and that's when I heard the gun go off. I thought-" she paused and swallowed hard, her voice too full of emotion to continue.

"So who shot him?" Janet asked, tiptoeing over to the doorway. She listened hard for a few seconds before peering around the door. She looked left, and then right, before turning back to me. "There's no one out here," she said, bewildered.

"We have to go," I told her, walking over to pull Rachel and Riley to their feet. "Someone heard that shot. They're going to be here any second."

"What if it's a trap?" Rachel asked, fearfully pulling Riley to her chest. Riley squirmed uncomfortably in her mother's grasp but didn't pull away.

I shrugged. "What if it's not?" Everyone was quiet, so I continued. "Janet made it out last time." Janet nodded, so I continued. "This might be our last chance. I don't know who is running this sick game but I'm certainly not going to wait around a second longer to find out."

With that, I began to march towards the door. I hesitated before taking a step into the hallway. Rachel was right — who knew what was out there waiting for us? Eventually, I worked up the courage to poke a foot out into the hall. When nothing happened to it, I peeked around the corner. Seeing nothing, I stepped forward, turned and began to hurry down the hallway, in the direction Riley claimed that Gregson had taken her before a large scary person appeared in the shadows. Maybe it had been Ernie. Maybe we had nothing to worry about. Maybe we'd actually get out of here.

I heard footsteps behind me. Whirling quickly, I took in the faces of Janet, Rachel and Riley, hot on my trail. Smiling, I continued to lead the charge. At the end of the hall, I could tell that I'd be forced to turn right or left. Without thinking, I quickly turned right and ran smack dab into a cocked gun. Figured.

The person holding the weapon was standing quietly, surrounded by darkness and shadows. My breathing quickened as my heart rate skyrocketed. The rest of my crew stopped abruptly, clutching one another in fear. "Marian," the person holding the gun finally said. The voice was male and sickly familiar. My mind raced with possibilities, but I didn't want to believe any of them. I pushed some hair out of my eyes and, in doing so, smeared the clotted blood from my injury across my forehead.

As my eyes adjusted to the darkness, realization dawned. I took a step back, raising my hands in a sign of defeat. "Frank," I said quietly.

He grinned a cold, evil grin. "Did you really just now figure it out?" he asked. "You didn't know all along that it was me?"

I shook my head. A sharp pain rippled through me and I tried not to faint from surprise, agony or both. Frank was my father's partner on the force for years. A stand-up citizen. He'd played football with my brother in the front yard every summer. He'd played tea party with my family on my birthday when I was five. He'd initiated the search for Riley along with my father almost immediately after hearing that she was missing. My eyes were seeing it, but my brain had yet to catch up. "Why?" I finally asked as he walked towards me. I continued walking slowly backwards, my hands raised. Briefly, I turned to glance at my companions. They were all just as surprised as I was. Especially Rachel, which was really throwing me off. If anyone would have known it was Frank all along, it would have been Rachel.

"I'd love to tell you everything," he said, his voice low and dangerous. His eyes glittered with something that I can only describe as mentally unhinged. "Really, I would. But let's get you back in your room first, hmm?" He looked around at my friends and waved the gun a bit. "All of you."

How did these people keep finding me? In the last month

and a half, I'd become a magnet for all sorts of gun toting crazies. I refused to turn my back on him. He'd probably shoot me the second he no longer had to look into my eyes. Instead, I walked backwards, cautiously watching Frank's hand. I nearly tripped over Ernie's body and worked hard not to gag as my shoes became drenched with his blood.

"You're disturbing the crime scene," Frank teased with a smile. Almost as quickly, he dropped the friendly mask and his face grew dark and angry. "Hurry up," he said, giving me a shove. I toppled backwards into our room, but Rachel and Janet caught my arms and hoisted me back to my feet.

"Did you shoot Ernie?" I asked incredulously, pointing to the body. My hand was shaking. "Did you do that?"

Frank began to laugh. It was a hollow, delirious sound that sent chills up and down every inch of my body. "That's your first question?"

"No, my first question was 'Why?'," I retorted.

Frank's face again lost any trace of amusement. He stepped closer but I held my ground. Rachel made a grab for Riley and pulled her close, while Janet stood just off to one side, ready to pounce. Frank was so close that his hot breath filled my nostrils. He smelled like cheap coffee and mustard-dipped pretzels. When he spoke, I noticed that his teeth were crooked, yellowed with age and poor dietary choices. "I'd forgotten how much I love your spirit, Marian," he said, gently running the gun barrel along my cheek and jawline before finally digging it into the fleshy part of my chin. His smile returned and he leaned close so that he could whisper into my ear. "Are you afraid?"

I wanted to pee. I wanted to run. I wanted to scream and plead, begging for my life. Instead, I set my jaw and took a deep breath. "No," I answered, praying he hadn't picked up on the shakiness of my voice.

"I sure would be," he answered, keeping the gun trained on my chin and moving behind me.

He began to pet my hair and I felt myself shake with disgust. The gun trained on my lower jaw kept me in place. He didn't seem to be in much of a hurry to lock all of us into the room again. Perhaps if I could get him talking, he'd be distracted enough that the others could escape. Swallowing hard, I took a long, quiet breath to calm my nerves. "Tell me why," I demanded again.

Frank seemed to think for a moment before he lowered the gun. I felt a weight lift as he took a few steps further into the room. His back was turned to all of us. "Don't even think about trying to run," he said lowly, reading my mind. "I am an excellent marksman. You'd be dead before you were halfway down the hall." That being said, he opened the gun and began counting bullets. "Five," he said with a satisfied grin. "Which gives me one extra shot."

I saw Riley's eyes widen and her grip around her mother tightened. The situation began to make me angry. Very, very angry. I was just about to tell Frank off when Janet beat me to it. "What kind of a sick person are you?" she spat, taking a step towards Frank. "At least let the girl go. She was never part of this to begin with."

"Never part of it?" Frank asked. He seemed surprised. Slowly, he started to chuckle. It turned into a throaty, maniacal laughter that haunted me from the inside out. Exchanging glances with Janet, I could tell she was equally disturbed. I stepped in front of Rachel and Riley. We were in the presence of a psycho and I didn't want my niece becoming more scarred than she probably already was. Frank's laughter stopped just as quickly as it had begun. Turning, he raised his gun and pointed it just over my shoulder at Rachel's head. "The girl was always part of it," he said darkly, "thanks to her mother."

"What the hell is that supposed to mean?" Janet asked, taking a step towards Rachel.

"Don't," Frank said, quickly moving the gun so that it was pointed at Janet. Her eyes widened and she froze. "Don't move," he told her. "Not one muscle." As he continued to level his gun at her forehead, a slow smile danced across his face. His eyes began to twinkle. "You're the cop," he said quietly. "The one from Georgia."

"Florida," she corrected.

"Whatever," he snapped. "You're a cop and you never figured all of this out?"

"You gave me the creeps when I first arrived," she replied. "Call it a woman's intuition."

"But I had a good cover, didn't I, Marian?" Frank asked as he took another step towards Janet. "You probably just dismissed her concerns for me. Why, I'm Don's partner. Old family friend. I even started the search for Riley to throw you idiots off my trail while I got things organized for myself to skip town." He now stood only about a foot away. He pressed the gun hard into Janet's skull but she continued to stare directly into his eyes, defiant. "I could kill you," he whispered.

"Then do it," she challenged.

I gulped. Janet was a total badass. I suppose you had to be, to some extent, when you were in such a male-centric field. Still, I'd never have anticipated this. She was cool as a cucumber, even in the face of death.

"When I grow up, I want to be just like you," I whispered, a small smile playing on my lips. I saw the corner of her mouth twitch slightly with a smile as she continued to challenge Frank with her stare. The air was thick with anticipation. I felt my heart hammering in my chest.

"That would be a hell of an ending, wouldn't it?" Frank asked. "You probably get off at night thinking about situations like this. Scenarios where you can play the hero. That really turns you on, doesn't it, Janice?"

"Janet," she corrected. "And yeah, Frankie, it really does."

Frank sneered and snapped the gun hard across Janet's face. She grunted and crumpled to the ground, lifeless. I started towards her but he turned and trained the gun on my chest. "Don't move," he whispered.

"I just want to check her," I said frantically. Desperate, I tried to peer around Frank's huge mass to see if my friend was still breathing.

"She's fine," he answered.

As if on cue, Janet moaned and rolled ever so slightly on the floor. "I didn't even hit her that hard." Frank turned and gave her a kick to the ribs. Her eyes shot open and she yelped, clutching her chest.

The gun no longer trained on me, I leapt forward and punched him right in the kidney. He wasn't phased but I didn't have any other shots. He was much taller than me, with quite a bit more mass around the middle. I couldn't even box his ears without a running leap. "Please just leave her alone," I insisted as he turned to stare at me.

Frank turned back to consider Janet for a moment before turning back to me. His gun remained lowered at his side, as he watched me, quietly. Finally he said, "Just because you asked nicely." He grinned. "And because you have such a mean punch. One more and you might knock me out cold." He laughed like he'd said something funny.

I breathed a sigh of relief and waited until he'd composed himself enough to speak. "Now tell me why," I whispered. "What did Riley have to do with any of this?"

Frank seemed to take joy in responding. "Rachel didn't tell you anything, did she?"

"Let's assume not," I said, narrowing my eyes. "Why don't you tell me everything?"

Frank grinned menacingly and looked over my shoulder to Rachel. "It would be so much better if she told you herself. I can fill in the holes."

Rachel was shaking her head, clutching Riley. "I- I can't," she said.

"Do it," said Frank, raising his gun towards Riley, "or the girl is the first to go."

Rachel's eyes widened in fear and she clutched her daughter tight. "Don't hurt her," she whispered.

"Then start talking," Frank bit back cooly.

Rachel took a deep breath. I turned to face her and saw the fear filling every inch of her being. "John and I needed money," she whispered to me. "The diner has been slow ever since the factory a town over had shut down. Gregson told me that he needed help getting his affairs in order, because he wanted to sell the house after Grace died. He'd pay me." She looked to Frank, who was staring at her, bored. He already knew where this was going. I continued to listen, captivated by the unfolding tale.

As it turned out, Gregson had boxes and boxes of books which he wished to sell. However, he would only sell to one store — The Quill in Chicago. It was where he and Grace had always sold their books for the best price, he'd promised Rachel. But he had gotten too old to make the drive, so his books just piled up. That's when Rachel began moving books for Gregson into the city, which he offered to pay her for. Or at least, she thought she was just moving books for Gregson. It was always odd to her that Gregson already had these boxes pre-packed. It was strange that she just handed over Gregson's taped up, cardboard boxes to Ernie at The Quill and that he simply handed her envelopes of cash, not even bothering to check the merchandise. Then again, Rachel never read and certainly never sold books on her own. Maybe that was just how things worked. Rachel wasn't one to ask many questions and Gregson knew it. He had targeted her.

One day, almost as if fate were playing its hand, one of the boxes Rachel picked up from Gregson's had ripped wide open in the middle of a Chicago street and all of the books fell out of the bottom. She hadn't noticed anything out of the ordinary until she went to pick up the contents and realized that they were hollow books filled with baggies of white powder.

Nervous, but deciding to carry out Gregson's wishes, Rachel had stacked everything neatly back into the box and repaired the tape as best she could. She took the box into Ernie's store and handed it over, as per usual. Ernie pulled some cash out of his drawer and tucked it into an envelope, just as he always had. Rachel had driven straight back to Gregson's. She didn't know to suspect that she'd been used as a flunky. Call her naive. Call her small-town. Given her upbringing, I couldn't blame her. Heck, I hadn't even known what marijuana smelled like until I was in college. My parents, both hippies before they'd had my brother and I, gave up every substance outside of the occasional cocktail while we were being raised. Rachel had not only grown up in a similar environment, she also wasn't quite as bright as the majority of the population. Which would explain her next move, thought by anyone else to be completely and totally stupid. She'd confronted Gregson. She'd demanded answers. She refused to give him the cash unless he explained what was going on. Worse, she threatened to tell everyone what he really did for a living.

Gregson, however, wasn't one to be pushed around. He'd been involved in the trade for years and had worked his way up the ladder, but he was getting old. He was tired of looking over his shoulder all the time. He was certainly too old to be offing people. Gregson wanted out of the business. But you don't just "get out" of drug trafficking. He needed a plan. He needed a lot of money. He'd needed to stay in the business for a while longer.

When Rachel confronted him, threatening to expose all of his hard work, Gregson saw his last few years going up in smoke unless he came up with a plan. The most obvious choice was to kill her. The second choice was to feign ignorance, but then Rachel would probably just insist that together they go to the cops. Gregson had suspected Frank as the head of the whole drug operation for a long time, even though he couldn't prove it. While Frank was retired, he stayed involved in the local department on a voluntary basis and there was no way he wouldn't hear something. Either way, it would be bad for both Gregson and Rachel if she told anyone. His third choice, and the one that made the most sense, was to bring Rachel into the business. It wouldn't be easy, so he'd played a dirty card. He threatened to kill Riley if Rachel so much as breathed a word to anyone about his involvement. He even had her convinced that my dad, her father-in-law, might not be a trustworthy cop. No wonder she hadn't told him everything from the beginning.

Once Gregson sufficiently scared the bejesus out of my sister-in-law, he'd begun to hatch a plan. He told his boss, whom he'd never even seen, but suspected was Frank, that he was bringing Rachel in to work as a mover.

The Feds were getting close to Gregson. Rachel could deter them for a while, working on his behalf and making him appear retired from the drug business, but that would eventually come to an end and he'd be arrested and jailed. Jail wasn't for Gregson. He'd never survive. The only other option was to escape.

Without Frank's knowledge or approval, Gregson had Rachel open up a bank account under her name — a move that would get him killed if Frank ever found out. The allure of escaping his crime-ridden life and starting over, however, was far too tempting. While he would have preferred opening a new account under his own name, it would raise red flags for the FBI, who had been monitoring him for months. Instead, Gregson fed Rachel bundles of cash to deposit into the secret bank account. When there was enough, he planned to have her wire it to an account in Europe, give her a percentage off the top, and run away to live out life on a beach.

It didn't matter that Rachel racked up several million dollars in the account in weeks. It didn't even matter that the bank she'd opened an account with was known for its shady business practices and was under scrutiny by the government. Rachel hadn't been on anyone's radar and no one knew she was Gregson's pawn. Plus, three million, while a lot to most of us, wasn't squat compared to other accounts at the bank. Chump change.

Rachel, however, had a scheme of her own. She was going to take her family and the money, and run, leaving Gregson to rot. The account, after all, was all in her name. She, John, Riley, me and my parents would all retire somewhere further south, holed up until it was safe to come out and all the major players that were playing Rachel for a fool were dead. She'd even bought the plane tickets. A pipe dream to be sure, convincing all of us to move to Costa Rica at the drop of a hat, but quite sweet, really.

Unfortunately, Gregson had caught on to her plan. It was time to show Rachel what he was capable of if she disobeyed him again. He'd used his men to kidnap Riley. His intent was to keep the little girl safe in a hotel somewhere in downtown Chicago until Rachel had been reasoned with. Rachel, he figured, didn't need to know that her daughter was sitting in a fluffy bed at The Ritz, watching ten dollar movies and snacking on Butterfingers.

That's when things started to go downhill for Gregson. His henchmen ultimately took orders from Frank. When Frank had called the night of Riley's kidnapping, needing someone "taken care of," Gregson's men had to explain that they were indisposed, having just stuffed Riley into their backseat. Frank demanded that the henchmen bypass the hotel and bring Riley straight to him. That's about the time he started suspecting something bigger was going on and began to sniff around.

Gregson, discovering that Riley was at the distribution warehouse in Chicago, rather than comfy in The Ritz, couldn't let Rachel know Riley was in any real danger or she'd go to the police for sure. He'd be arrested or worse. He convinced Rachel that Riley was being kept somewhere safe and that she only had to play along to get Riley back. That's when he came up with the idea for a ransom note. He'd hoped a nondescript note would buy him time, but all it did was bring in reinforcements. Rachel, brilliantly, had set the ransom to match Riley's birthday, a fact Gregson didn't find out until later. Maybe she wasn't unintelligent, maybe she was just above us all.

When my friends and I came to town and jumped onto Gregson's trail a little too quickly for his liking, he'd had Rachel plant another note, proposing a drop, hoping to buy himself time to make another move. Rachel, still fearing for Riley's life and willing to do anything to get her back, had played along with the whole thing. Having never met Mika, James or Janet before, she'd had no idea if they were trustworthy. Gregson had her good and brainwashed. She wasn't willing to risk Riley's life by giving anything away. Additionally, she refused to tell Addison or I, knowing we'd relay any information back to the others. It explained her chilly demeanor towards us upon our discovery of her secret accounts. After all, to discover something like that so quickly, one of us had to know Gregson, someone involved in the drug ring, or both. As it turned out, my friends were just very good at what they did. What may have taken others several days, took us only several hours. Ernie being a total moron had played a significant role in our overall success.

From there, it had just been one mistake after another, which had somersaulted into all of us being held here. "And unfortunately," Frank said upon conclusion of Rachel's story, "I'm going to have to kill all of you now. You can thank Greg for that one."

"Gregory!" Frank roared. You got the feeling that people did what he said.

A few seconds later, Gregson scurried around the corner and into the room. His head was bowed down to the floor and his shoulders were hunched, as if he knew something horrible was coming. "Yes?" he asked timidly.

"Kill them," Frank said simply, handing Gregson his gun.

Even Janet, who was still sprawled out on the floor, dropped her jaw. "Excuse me?" Gregson asked, clutching the cold, hard barrel.

Frank's face grew dark and dangerous. "You heard me," he said lowly. "I want you to kill them. All of them. Don't come out of here until they're dead." With that, Frank strode towards the door. "I'll be watching," he said, pointing towards the ceiling in the darkness — I assumed at a camera that we couldn't see. Then, he stepped out of the room and shut and locked the door behind him.

Gregson may have had the gun, but he had three pissed off adult women staring him down and no henchmen. Fate was finally on our side. I'd have gladly taken a bullet if it meant taking out this jerk once and for all. How dare he threaten Rachel like that? How dare he involve my family? Gregson could sense our hatred. He kept the gun firmly at his side and looked from one of us to the next. "I tried to help you," he pled. "I feel so badly about all of this. I just wanted out. I've never killed a woman. I've never hurt a kid." He looked sympathetically at Riley. "It goes against my good moral judgement."

I looked up towards the ceiling, where I finally caught a glimpse of the camera. It was tiny — no larger than a bottle cap. Pointing, I looked at Gregson. "Can he hear us or just see us? It's time you were honest."

"He can't hear you," Gregson assured me.

"How long until he makes it back to the live feed to check up on you?" Janet asked, rolling onto her knees. I hurried over to help her stand.

"He'll go get a cup of coffee first," Gregson said, grinning. "Unfortunately, he'll have to wait until it finishes brewing."

"How do you know he'll wait?" Rachel asked curiously.

"He'll wait," Gregson promised.

"Can you get us out of here?" I asked. Maybe now that his own life was in danger, he'd help us.

Gregson hesitated only a second. "No," he admitted, turning his gaze back to the floor. "Frank took my key."

"Then you better start talking," I said angrily. "Why did you do this?"

"You heard why!" he cried. "I was outside listening the whole time! No one was supposed to get hurt," he assured us. "I didn't even want to be in this business in the first place. Grace said-"

"Grace?" I asked sharply. "Your wife?" Gregson nodded. As it turned out, Grace's brother had been involved in the Polish mob ring in Chicago. "The Polish mob?" I asked skeptically.

Gregson nodded. "It's a real thing, I swear!" From there, he told us that, when Grace's brother had been killed, Grace confessed that the family money she claimed to have — the money that had sustained them for years — actually was funneled to her by her brother. They were broke. She begged Gregson to take her brother's place and had just the connections to get him started. Gregson had been laid off at the factory a few months prior and had been unable to find work again since. He'd agreed to make them a few dollars working for the mob distributing drugs down in Chicago until a real job came along. He loved Grace. He hated to see her unhappy.

Only another job had never come along. He'd gotten in deeper and deeper with the Polish mob, working his way up in the dangerous, lucrative world of drugs. Polish gangsters, he assured us, were just as ferocious as any other gangster in the big city. Personally, I had a hard time picturing a Polish gangster, but I suppose weirder things had happened in the world.

Eventually Grace died, which was about the same time Gregson decided that he wanted out of the business for good. We knew the rest of the story. "I tried to get all of you out," he assured us again. "You think I'm dumb enough to leave a door unlocked?"

"You seem dumb enough for a lot of things," Riley quipped. Rachel shushed her immediately.

"You did that?" Janet asked, incredulous.

"Of course I did," Gregson snapped. "How many times do I have to say it? I didn't mean for any of this to happen. You're not even my prisoners, technically! You're his!"

"I just didn't realize-" I started.

"Yeah, well, you've underestimated me a lot over the years, haven't you Moyer?" he sneered.

"He has a point," Rachel chimed in.

"Thank you, Rachel," Gregson said kindly.

"Oh, shut up, Gregson," I snapped. "What are we going to do? As soon as Frank realizes you haven't shot us all dead, he'll finish the job himself."

Gregson shook his head. "He won't," he assured us quietly.

"Because you seem to know so much," I said sarcastically. My head was once again pounding with pain. It wasn't completely unbearable but I knew it would be soon.

"Frank has never killed anyone," Gregson said simply. "He's knows the penalty under the law for that."

"You've known the man personally as the head of the Polish mob since when?" I cried. "Yesterday? He killed Ernie!"

"He didn't," Gregson assured me.

"Frank never did admit to killing Ernie," Rachel said.

"That's true, he didn't," Janet added.

"Well then, who did?" I asked.

Gregson shrugged. "I just know it wasn't Frank. And anyway, I was in the control room with him when the gun went off. That's when Frank took my gun and my key. He told me to wait for him, but after he left, I crept into the hallway so that I could hear everything happening down here. I didn't want anyone misconstruing my side of the story. You can see how that might happen."

I felt my heart swell with hope. If Frank hadn't shot Ernie, and Gregson hadn't shot Ernie, then perhaps we had an ally among us after all.

"Hey," I asked Gregson nonchalantly. "Where's that other guy? The one that you didn't like?" If the other person on our side was Richard, I wanted to have a location on him. He might be able to help us bust out of here.

"I shot him out back," Gregson said with a casual shrug.

"What?" I squeaked. "Why?"

"I don't know, I didn't like the guy," Gregson muttered. "He just rubbed me wrong. I'm not sure who brought him in but the guy just couldn't cut me a break. I'm old. I'm slow. He just wanted everything now, now, now. Frank put him under my charge a few weeks ago. I didn't need him, so..." Gregson mimicked shooting himself with his pistol.

"What's Frank going to say about that?" I asked, wide-eyed.

"Frank'll be none too pleased," Gregson retorted. "So we'd best start thinking of what we're going to do when he comes storming through that door."

"Why do you want to help us all of a sudden?" Janet asked. "You've been giving off a lot of mixed signals."

Gregson's face hardened. "I told you, I've never shot a lady." He looked to me. "Thought I'd have to today, if it came down to me or you. And who knows? For the three of you pain in the asses, I might be willing to make an exception. Especially you," he said wagging the gun at Rachel. "Then Miss Riley and I can head south. Make a stop at Disney World before I take her on a boat over to Europe, where she'll get the finest education boarding school can offer."

Riley's eyes grew wide with excitement. "Disney?" she asked, turning to her mother. Rachel just sighed, heavily.

"You're the reason I'm in this mess," Gregson muttered to Rachel.

"YOU'RE the reason you're in this mess," I retorted. "You and Grace!"

"Don't speak her name!" Gregson screamed. The room grew deathly silent while Gregson stared me down. When I refused to break eye contact, he growled at me instead.

Just then, we heard a key slide into the lock. "Party's over," Janet whispered. Turning to Gregson, she tilted her head in thought. "What's the likelihood he grabbed another gun?"

The locked clicked and the door began to swing open. "Slim to none," Gregson answered quickly, the fear on his face evident. "Why do you ask?"

"Because we're busting out of here," I answered, smiling

at Janet who nodded back.

The door swung wide and behind it stood Frank, angry as a bull. His face was red, his scalp was red, even his hands were red. "Gregson!" he began to roar.

Before the entirety of the word was out of his mouth, I charged at him with a loud battle cry. Completely stunned, Frank froze. I bowled straight through him, knocking him to the ground. "How's that for a punch?" I cried as his head made a sickening cracking sound against the wall. I didn't wait around to see if it had knocked him out. "Hurry!" I cried to the group, motioning down the hall.

Riley was out first, followed quickly by Rachel and then Janet. "Go on," Gregson told me. "I have the gun- I'll take up the rear. Let's get you gals out of here." I nodded and plunged down the hallway after the others. Running was not proving beneficial to a head injury but I didn't have much of a choice. Who knew who would come after us following that commotion? At the end of the hall, we turned left, finding ourselves stuck behind a locked door. "No! He's locked it! This is the way out!" Gregson hollered.

"Then we have to find another way," I answered, tugging on Janet's shirt to turn her around. "Let's go!" We raced towards the other end of the hallway. I allowed myself a quick glance towards where we'd escaped and saw Frank still laying motionless on the floor.

At the other end of the hallway was an open door that led us into what I can only assume was the control room.

There were lights and switchboards and televisions everywhere. I studied the screens but there didn't seem to be anyone running after us in that moment which I took as a good sign. No one knew we had escaped. Not even the guards.

Gregson sucked in a sharp breath. "Hold on just a cotton pickin' minute," he said, squinting hard at one of the screens that looked like it was focused outside. He seemed to become lost in thought for a moment and then started to nod to himself. "Yeah. Yeah, that's right. I shot Dick- right here. Right here in the yard, I shot him. Dead bodies can't just get up and walk away!"

"Live ones can," came a low voice behind us.

As if on cue, we all spun around to face the voice. There stood Richard, smugly aiming his gun at Gregson's forehead. "Richard!" I cried happily. "You're alive!"

"And just saving your ass again, Moyer," he grinned. "You didn't really think I had crossed over to the dark side, did you?"

"I guess I shouldn't have," I smiled back. "But how are you alive? Gregson said he killed you."

"I thought I had," Gregson mumbled.

Richard sneered. "Drop your weapon or I'll shoot you right here, right now. And I wouldn't have any problems falling asleep tonight."

Gregson seemed to take in the situation and begrudgingly dropped his gun to the ground. I scrambled to pick it up and quickly handed it off to Janet. I've never shot anything, not even targets at a practice facility. If something happened, I trusted Janet in the clutch. "But really, how did you survive?" I asked. "Inquiring minds want to know."

Bemused, Richard used his free hand to unbutton the top half of his shirt. Pulling it away, it revealed a kevlar vest. "Bullet proof," he said, patting it happily.

"I'm surprised they have one large enough to fit you," Gregson balked.

Turning to Gregson, Richard grinned. "It's amazing what money can buy these days. A word of advice- if you're going to shoot someone, it's always best to do it execution style. You know, in case they're a cop."

"I'll remember that for next time," Gregson assured him, curling back his upper lip.

"Do you know a way out of here, Richard?" I asked, suddenly excited.

"I do," he answered. "Turn around."

Janet shook her head. "It's just a control room."

Richard shook his head and grinned. "Oh, it's so much more than a control room. Push on that panel. No, no- the one under the main switchboard." As Janet did so, the panel popped further in and then pushed itself out. "Now slide it to the side," Richard told her.

Janet did as she was told and then began to laugh in delight. "It's a staircase!" she crowed.

"How did you know that was in here?" Gregson asked Richard, appalled. "You haven't even been working here all that long."

"Your whole operation has been under scrutiny for years," Richard assured him. "This isn't the only emergency exit Frank has." For a moment, Richard looked perplexed. "Speaking of, where is Frank?"

Riley giggled. "Aunt Em took care of him."

Richard looked at me curiously, but I just shrugged.

"Well, let's get you all going then," he said, gesturing towards the exit. He put a hand on Gregson's shoulder. "You can walk with me."

Gregson sighed, "You wouldn't try to incapacitate a feeble old man, would you? I'm almost 80 years old. I'm delicate."

Richard gave Gregson a light shove. "Shut up and walk."

Janet took up the lead. Slowly, we felt our way down the damp, earthy walls and into total blackness. "I can't see anything," Janet called back to us. Suddenly a bright light cut through the shadow. I turned to see Richard using the flashlight on his phone. "That works," Janet replied happily.

My head was beginning to pound. I needed a place to rest. I needed medicine. Mostly, I just needed a Reese's Peanut Butter Cup. Those tended to resolve all of my issues, no matter their size. I leaned against the cool wall as a cold sweat began to set in. It wasn't much further. I just had to survive a little bit longer. I could do it.

As if in a dream, we stumbled towards what looked like a ladder. At the top of the ladder, slits of light pressed through wooden boards. I turned curiously to Richard, but he just clicked off his flashlight and continued to hold his gun steady on Gregson. Janet began to scale the ladder, pushing her way higher and higher. When she reached the top, she hesitated for only a moment before bursting through the ceiling. The rest of us followed suit.

It was a secret exit, located amidst a stack of wooden

crates in what appeared to be a muddy lot behind a warehouse.

Off in the distance, a dog began to bark loudly. "Oh, no," Janet groaned. "We'll never get out of here with that horse after us!"

The barks became louder and the six of us stood, frozen in fear. We didn't want to be split up, but if we didn't start running wildly in different directions, the monster would probably eat all of us in one razor-toothed gulp. A huge hunk of fur and slobber came barreling around the corner. It was, as I feared, the beast from outside The Quill. He stopped suddenly when he saw Janet and I, almost as if he were surprised. Then, just as suddenly, he ducked his head and stalked towards us slowly, growling and snapping. "Oh, God," Gregson whispered, pressing himself backwards into Richard's chest. "This is it! I survive the mob all these years, just to get eaten by a dog!"

"Thor!" we heard a male voice call. The dog paused, perking up instantly. He looked left, then right, searching for the voice. "Thor!" the voice called again. It sounded familiar but I couldn't quite place it. The dog, however, leapt in joy and then began to whine, walking back and forth, watching us. He wanted his master but he dared not leave us behind all suddenly free to escape. He began to bark, willing his master to come to him.

We heard footsteps crunching in the gravel as the voice drew closer. "You've got to be kidding," Janet muttered as Shannon rounded the corner. "Don't move!" she screamed at him, raising the gun. "Don't move an inch or I'll shoot you."

The dog began to bark wildly at Janet, lunging but never moving close enough to bite her. He was waiting for a signal. If Shannon so much as flinched, Janet was going down before she could get a shot off. I was just sure of it. Then I'd have to pick up the gun and hope that Richard could fire his off before I had to.

"Woah!" Shannon cried, his eyes widening. He looked at Richard, who had started laughing. "Put the gun down, Janet."

"How the hell do you know my name?" she asked, wide-eyed. The dog continued to bark, angry and unafraid. She turned and pointed her gun at the dog. "Shut up!" she cried.

"Quiet, Thor!" Shannon said sternly. The dog whined and then was quiet, sitting back on his haunches, licking his lips nervously, looking from Janet to his master and back to Janet.

"Well trained dog," I muttered. "I'll give you that."

"Now will you put the gun down?" Shannon asked as Janet swung back towards him.

She laughed, a high nervous titter. "Why should I?"

"Because he's a cop," Richard responded. "Put your gun down, Janet."

Janet and I were dumbfounded. "A cop?" we asked simultaneously. Janet dropped the gun to her side, removing her finger from the trigger.

Shannon still held one hand up in a defensive position. With the other, he tugged at his pocket for a few seconds before pulling out a leather wallet. He flipped it open to reveal his credentials. "FBI Agent Shannon Montgomery Shultz," he grunted. Janet inched closer before warily glancing at his ID and badge.

"But you look just like the rest of the henchmen around here," I said incredulously.

"Why do you think he was perfect to go in undercover?" Richard asked. "He looked just like the stupid triplets."

"I convinced my boss to bring in Richard a few days ago," Shannon continued. "We've been watching Frank a long time, in association with the Chicago Police Department. Had to wait until we had enough evidence to bring him down. Unfortunately, he's known for not being one to kill people himself. He gets his men to do it."

"Told you so," Gregson sang smugly. Richard knocked him over the back of the head.

"A lot of people want to see Frank dead," Shannon assured us. "And don't get me wrong, because I think he's scum, but I want to see him squirm his way through a federal trial. Maybe spend a few months in lockdown. Problem was, we needed to get him on some bigger charges before anything long-term would stick to his sentencing. Attempted murder, maybe."

"Well we have all of that on camera," Janet told him. "He told Gregson to take care of us. Must have seen on the surveillance videos that we were still alive. Charged in, mad as hell." She paused. "We were afraid for our lives," she added with a smile.

"Where is Frank, anyway?" Shannon asked, looking around us. "He's surprisingly fast for his size. How is he not out here by now?"

"Knocked unconscious still, I think," I said with a shrug. "I kind of accidentally introduced his head to a wall."

"Atta girl," Richard told me with a light slap to the shoulder. It caused a sharp pain to spring through my neck and head and I winced. "Sorry," Richard muttered.

Just then, we heard the sound of cars crunching through the gravel behind us. Our entire group stood in the center of three large warehouses. The sky was a late afternoon blue, dulled by wisps of clouds that slowly sailed across the sky. "About time they got here," Shannon muttered under his breath.

Four nondescript navy blue cars whipped around the corner and squealed to a stop. Out stepped just over a half dozen stone-faced men in plain clothes. "I called you assholes 20 minutes ago," Shannon called, his voice not even the slightest bit irritated. A smile danced on his lips. He had a gorgeous smile. And his arms filled out that black shirt quite nicely. I found my head tilting sideways, catching a glimpse of his adorable bubble butt as he walked towards his friends.

"Two, Marian. You're already dealing with two men," Janet reminded me, shaking me out of my daydream.

"Had to stop for doughnuts," one of the men called to

Shannon, causing everyone to burst into laughter. The one who made the doughnut comment stopped short when he saw Riley. "Hey! This the girl?"

"That's the one," Richard shouted.

The man came over and knelt in front of Riley, who was clutching at Rachel's shirt. "You've had a lot of people out looking for you, young lady."

"Me?" Riley asked, pointing to herself. She checked behind her, on the off chance that someone was standing there that she didn't know about.

"Yes, you," the man answered.

Riley placed a hand on her hip and smiled. "People like you?" she asked with a bit of sass. With that crooked smile and cornstalk colored hair, the man couldn't help but smile back. He was under her spell. We all were.

I heard the sound of another car approaching. No sooner did it zip around the corner and park than the man told Riley, "Well yes, me. And them, too." He motioned at the car. All four doors of the car were thrown open. My father, my mother, Addison, Rory, Mika, James, John and even Janet's husband spilled out and raced towards us. There was also a woman I didn't recognize, whom I could only assume was Carly Ipson. She was short with long red hair and spunky freckles splattered across her pale, thin face and arms.

I'm not sure who got to who first. I don't remember who I kissed or hugged, or whose shirt I began to cry into. I just knew that I was finally safe. We were all back together.

The nightmare was over.

Unfortunately, I hadn't killed Frank. I'd only managed to give him a pretty major concussion. He was facing some pretty serious charges, now that the law had finally caught up to him.

The rest of the police cavalry showed up not long after my family and friends arrived. Frank, Gregson, the menacing bodyguards and a few other people I'd never seen before, were dragged off in cuffs.

I got a ride to the city in the back of an ambulance and spent a few days in the hospital, where my family took turns regaling me with the tale of what happened after Janet and I had fallen off the radar.

Addison had made the call to Richard, who was already deep in the trenches. When Addison mentioned that Janet and I were searching for my niece, Riley, Richard immediately knew that she was the kid Frank was keeping locked up in the warehouse. He'd made Addison swear that she would keep Janet and I out of it. The situation was dangerous. If we were caught, we likely wouldn't make it out alive.

Richard hung up with Addison and made a call to Shannon. Shannon, of course, recognized us from having just been in the bookstore and almost immediately called his people. Ernie somehow heard part of the conversation and alerted Gregson that we were not the new people he'd been informed would be coming in — no one seemed to know who said "new people" even were — but, rather, we were outsiders. Realizing his mistake, Ernie had begged Gregson for help cleaning up the mess. Gregson, who seemed to have made all the wrong contacts in the mob, told one of his henchmen the whole story, who then told someone else, who ultimately told Frank.

Frank sent out his boys to bring Janet and I in. He figured that if he could just keep the two of us quiet, he could make the whole thing go away. He was going to kill Gregson, force Rachel to withdraw the money in the account Gregson had made her open, then basically take all four of his hostages — Riley, Rachel, Janet and myself — and shove us off a cliff. He'd fly to the Cayman Islands and live the rest of his life in retirement before anyone suspected his involvement. Unfortunately for Frank, he didn't know that there were people on the inside of his operation.

Richard had been the one to shoot Ernie and then had gone back into the shadows, waiting to make his next move when we'd need him most. Ernie had been on his way in to kill us.

Shannon apologized profusely for not filling Janet in when he found her behind the warehouse. There was no place to take her without blowing his cover, as we were in the middle of nowhere. He couldn't risk her knowing that they were about to bring Frank down. Therefore, he had to return her to the warehouse and bide his time. He'd hoped that by splitting us up, it would be easier to sneak us out when the time came. When the guard tried to take advantage of Janet, however, Shannon changed his mind and decided that there was strength in numbers, returning her to be with me.

My friends and family all stayed at a nearby hotel until my hospital release. When the day finally arrived for me to go home, my parents, brother, sister-in-law and niece arrived to bid me a fond farewell. Thankfully, my brother got the whole story from Rachel and Richard. While he was upset that Rachel hadn't confided in him, he understood that she had only wanted to keep her family safe and was able to forgive her.

I also got to see Janet and her husband one last time. They had a flight back to Florida scheduled that very afternoon. "Thanks for everything," I whispered to Janet as we hugged goodbye. "You're the best."

"That's what friends are for," she assured me with a grin.

"I think this went above and beyond the call of friendship," I laughed.

"In that case, you owe me one, sister."

"So long as next time, it's in Florida," I joked. "I'm so tired of winter."

"You've always got a room at our place," her husband,

Rob, answered, squeezing my shoulder. I smiled at him, knowing the offer was genuine.

Addison and Rory drove me home to Milwaukee, with James and Mika following close behind. When we arrived at my apartment, Rory reached for my bag in the backseat, but I stopped him. "I've got it," I promised.

"Marian, I can-" he started, but I shushed him.

"I have a head injury," I assured him. "I'm not dead."

"No," he said with a grin, "I guess you're not."

"Call me later, then?" Addison asked.

"Count on it," I promised her.

James and Mika both parked outside my building but I simply shook my head at them. "Please." I wanted to be alone. In my own apartment. With my fish, Fred, and a giant glass of wine. Maybe a pile of peanut butter cups. I had a king size still hidden in the freezer somewhere, I was sure.

I walked in the front door and immediately dropped my overnight bag to the floor. Closing the door and locking it behind me, I leaned up against the wall, exhausted.

After a few moments, I began flipping on light switches. When I came to the lamp that was on the desk by Fred, I gently tapped the glass and waggled a finger to say "hello." Fred looked displeased. I couldn't blame him. He hadn't eaten in days. With this in mind, I dropped an extra large pinch of dried flakes into his bowl. He swam at them, greedily taking huge mouthfuls.

A few minutes later, I was in the kitchen, pouring a glass of fruity white wine when my phone began to ring. I checked the caller ID and smiled, answering with a happy "hey there."

"I got the feeling that you wanted to be alone tonight," said a familiar, sexy male voice, "but I just can't help myself from trying one last time before I go home." A pause. "I missed you."

"Did you?" I asked, flirtatiously.

"I did," he answered solemnly. "I was so worried about you, Marian."

"Well, in that case," I said, taking a sip of wine, "you'd best go ahead and come up. Just to make sure that I really am okay."

THE END

Allison Janda is a writer with New York Times bestseller dreams. She currently resides in Nebraska with her two dogs, one of which acts more like a cat.

Visit her today (or tomorrow, if you're in a hurry right now) at:

AllisonJanda.com
Twitter: @AllisonJanda
Facebook.com/AllisonJJanda

An excerpt from Book #3 in the Marian Moyer series: Scandal, Temptation & a Taste of Flan

Later, I was sitting alone in the studio. Carmen had washed up, changed and headed back to her hotel. For some reason, her limousine had disappeared, so Addison, jaw tight and angry, agreed to take the colorfully spoken Bolivian back herself.

I was flipping through the digital screen on my camera for the hundredth time, admiring just how perfectly the shoot had turned out, when I heard footsteps behind me. "Tarp is cleaned up and drying. Dressing room is wiped down. Do you need anything else before I head out for the afternoon?" Rory asked kindly, coming up behind me. Looking at the photos over my shoulder, he whistled low and long. "Don't tell Addison I said this, but Carmen is even more beautiful in person than she is on the big screen."

"In appearance maybe," I answered. "But her personality sucks." Shutting off the camera, I flipped open a side compartment and pulled out the memory stick. "All yours," I told him. "Use appropriately."

"I'll get these uploaded first thing tomorrow," he promised, ignoring me and tucking the small drive into his shirt pocket.

I heard my phone vibrating in my purse. Standing from the stool and stretching, I hurried over and pulled it from the side pocket. "Hey," I said to Addison after checking the caller ID. "Everything okay? I was expecting you back to the studio already. Rory and I are getting ready to head out." There was a loud sniffle and then a gut-wrenching sob from the other side of the phone. "Addie?" I asked, alarmed. Rory's head snapped up and he looked at me curiously, the concern in my voice evident. "What happened? What's wrong? Where are you?"

"The hotel," she gasped out between sobs and sniffs. "Carmen's dead and- oh, Marian, I think I need a lawyer."

• • •

To purchase Book #3 and stay up-to-date about all future releases, visit AllisonJanda.com/books right now!

68834829R00149

Made in the USA
Lexington, KY
20 October 2017

ME